Love and War

Love and War

Barbara Cartland

G.K. Hall & Co. • Chivers Press
Thorndike, Maine USA   Bath, England

This Large Print edition is published by G.K. Hall & Co., USA, and by Chivers Press, England.

Published in 1998 in the U.S. by arrangement with International Book Marketing, Ltd.

Published in 1998 in the U.K. by arrangement with Cartland Promotions.

U.S.   Softcover   0-7838-0311-7   (Paperback Series Edition)
U.K.   Hardcover   0-7540-3505-0   (Chivers Large Print)
U.K.   Softcover   0-7540-3506-9   (Camden Large Print)

The text of this Large Print edition is unabridged.
Other aspects of the book may vary from the original edition.

Set in 16 pt. Plantin.

Printed in the United States on permanent paper.

British Library Cataloguing in Publication Data available

Library of Congress Cataloging in Publication Data

Cartland, Barbara, 1902–
    Love and war / a new Camfield novel of love / by Barbara Cartland.
        p.   cm.
    ISBN 0-7838-0311-7   (lg. print : sc : alk. paper)
    1. Large type books.   I. Title.
[PR6005.A765L615   1998]
823´.912—dc21   98-26225

Author's Note

The late Sir Arthur Bryant in his book *The Age of Elegance* describes with his usual brilliance the suffering and the privation of the Army in Portugal, in the early 1800's.

The advance was slow over the mountains where guns had never been carried before and those who returned to England wounded resented bitterly the frivolity in Social London.

In a day when there was no television and no newspaper reporting, it was difficult for those people in the circle of the Prince Regent to understand what was happening in Europe.

However in the Winter following the Spring in which this novel is situated the first victories of Wellington's army against Napoleon sent:

"The heart of the British people rocketing, from the Prince Regent who hugged the Speaker when he announced the news, to the smock-frocks around the ale-house fire, they were kept that Winter in a state of continual excitement.

"On October 18th a chaise and four with a flag waving from the window, dashed on to the Horse Guards Parade with the news of Wellington's crossing of the Bidassoa.

"A fortnight later the Tower salvoes proclaimed the victory of Leipzig."

There was still a long way to go to Waterloo but with other countries joining Wellington's Army victory was in sight.

chapter one

1813

Gina walked back into the Morning-Room and thought how pretty it was.

It was lovely to be home after being so long at her Finishing School.

She was enjoying everything she saw in the house.

She walked across the floor to the window.

At the back there was a garden, which at the moment was filled with flowers, and the trees were in blossom.

Her Father, when she was still quite small, had built a small fountain in the centre of the green lawn.

It was now throwing its water in a rainbow of iridescent colours up to the sky.

She sat down in the corner of the window, where there was a comfortable window-seat under the long Georgian panes.

She squeezed herself into one corner so that she could see a particularly pretty bed of roses which were her Mother's favourite.

She remembered as a child excitedly picking the first bud in the summer.

She had then run upstairs to give it to her Mother.

"It looks like you, Mama," she cried, and knew the compliment pleased her.

Lady Langdale at the time had been one of the greatest beauties of London.

She had made her debut with a number of her contemporaries, but had stood out amongst them.

Everyone admired her.

No one had been surprised when, at the end of her first Season, when she was just eighteen, she had married Lord Langdale.

He was an extremely eminent Statesman.

He had been very much older than his bride.

Yet because he was rich and distinguished, no one had questioned the disparity in their ages.

Gina had been heartbroken when, just over a year ago, her Father, who was nearly seventy, had died of a heart attack.

She had loved being with him and talking to him.

It was he who had insisted that she have a very comprehensive education.

It was certainly something that few English girls were having.

The War had prevented those who were older from going abroad.

It was Lord Langdale who had discovered there was an outstandingly good Finishing School for Ladies of Quality outside Bath.

He had sent Gina there just before he died.

Because it was a long and difficult journey she had not returned home until now.

Before that she had had Governesses and Tutors in a large number of subjects.

Her Mother had realised that Lord Langdale was giving his daughter almost a boy's education.

It was of course because he did not have a son.

Lady Langdale had been intelligent enough not to interfere.

She said nothing when Gina had Tutors in most European languages and also learnt Latin.

She had made, however, a little murmur of disagreement when Lord Langdale had insisted on Gina learning French.

"But, Darling," she argued, "we are at War with France. Surely she should not learn the language of our enemies?"

"To defeat the French, not only in War but in Peace," Lord Langdale replied, "we must learn their language. It is a great mistake not to be able to speak the language of every country one visits."

He spoke prophetically as he went on:

"I feel sure that when hostilities cease and Napoleon Bonaparte is defeated, people will visit France as they have done in the past."

Lady Langdale gave a little cry of protest.

"After the appalling way they have behaved," she said, "I could never speak to a Frenchman again."

Lord Langdale had not replied.

As a Statesman he was aware that diplomatically it would be impossible, once Napoleon was defeated, not to acknowledge France as an important country in Europe.

Gina therefore learnt French from a French teacher.

In the same way she had learnt the languages of other European countries that her Father had told her about.

"You have travelled so much, Papa," she said. "When I am grown up, will you take me with you?"

"Of course I will, my Dearest," he answered. "But I am sure that you will marry someone who will want to show you the beauty of Rome and the glory of Greece himself."

"I would rather go with you, Papa," Gina said firmly.

Her Father had smiled, but a little wistfully.

He had realised he was getting old.

He wondered how many years he would have with his entrancing and adorable daughter.

She was very beautiful.

This might have been expected, seeing how beautiful her Mother was.

At the same time he thought, but did not say so, that her beauty was more human, more engaging than that of his wife.

Lady Langdale was a classical beauty.

Everyone who saw her compared her with the Greek statues of Aphrodite or Artemis.

Perhaps, although it was something he would never admit, Lord Langdale sometimes found her rather dull.

When it came to talking of Politics or of the Diplomatic Missions which he undertook on behalf of the Prime Minister, she had nothing to say.

It was understandable, but he was determined that his daughter should be attractive not only because of her beauty but also because of her brains.

Gina had left school with the praise of the Headmistress ringing in her ears.

She had a whole pile of prizes for almost every subject that had been taught.

On her Father's instructions she had studied much that was outside the normal curriculum.

As there was no competition in these particular subjects, the teachers had themselves given her books which they inscribed "To my Most Brilliant Pupil."

"Mama will be proud," Gina thought, as she was travelling back to London.

Then she knew that her Mother would not be interested in her academic progress as her Father would have been.

Eventually she reached London.

It had been a long and tiring journey with a constant change of horses.

She found that everything in the house and the garden reminded her of her Father.

It was bad enough in London.

But she shrank from going to their Country House.

The stables would feel empty without him!

Her Mother disliked riding, so she would have to ride alone over the Estate which had been her Father's delight.

There was only one thing he had regretted.

Because he was so much in demand in London, he could not spend as much time as he wished in the country.

Gina now thought that it would be difficult to get her Mother away from London.

She had so many Social engagements with the *Beau Ton.*

Lady Langdale had of course been in mourning for a year.

She had however written to her daughter to say that she was now invited to quiet Dinner Parties.

While she would not attend Balls she would entertain at home.

There was a constant stream of visitors to their house in Berkeley Square.

"I am of course longing to see you, my Dearest," she had written in her last letter, "and the first thing we must do is to buy you some attractive clothes. I am sure that the shops in Bath do not in any way compare with Bond Street."

Gina, actually, had very good taste and she was not certain that this was true.

Her Father had given her a very generous allowance which was continued after his death.

She had bought some very attractive dresses and evening-gowns in Bath.

She understood, however, that as her Mother

adored shopping, she would want her to spend a great deal of time in shops.

But Gina was also anxious to see the Museums and Galleries that had opened in London while she had been away.

She was hoping that, though His Royal Highness the Prince Regent was not interested in young girls, her Mother would somehow get her invited to Carlton House.

The predilection of the Prince Regent for the Arts was well-known in Bath.

Every new purchase he made of pictures, statues and other objects was reported in the local newspapers.

"I want to see his Chinese Music Room," Gina thought.

She wondered if perhaps amongst her other languages she should have learnt Chinese.

She had arrived in London only yesterday evening.

Her Mother was giving a Dinner Party.

So Gina had only a few minutes alone with her before she had to change into her evening-gown.

Because she was tired she had gone to bed early.

She hoped she would have a long talk with her Mother this morning.

After Lady Langdale was called, Gina had gone to her bedroom.

Her Mother however was still too sleepy to listen to what she had to say.

"I will get up, Darling," she said, "and come downstairs. Then we can really have a cosy gossip together."

Gina agreed.

She had taken the opportunity of going into the Drawing-Room, her Father's Study and the Library.

She wanted to see what alterations had been made.

Of course, it made her think back to the happy times she had spent in these rooms in the past.

In the Study she felt the tears come into her eyes.

She remembered how often she had seen her Father sitting at his flat-topped desk coping with piles of papers.

They either concerned his activities in the House of Lords or the many committees of which he was a member.

The room, she thought, was redolent of him.

The Chippendale bookcase was filled with books they both enjoyed.

There was a magnificent picture of a winter landscape by Van Den Neer over the fireplace.

On one of the other walls were two of Stubbs's most outstanding pictures of horses.

A Gentleman holding his horse was Gina's favourite.

There were so many other familiar objects which brought back memories of the past.

Her Father's duelling-pistols were in their polished mahogany box.

There was the statue of Apollo he had brought back from Greece.

Then there were a dozen other gifts or purchases from almost every country in Europe.

"You must hate the War," she had said once to her Father, "because it confines you in England."

"There are many things in my own country which delight me," Lord Langdale replied. "The most important, my Dearest, being you."

He kissed her.

Then they had plunged into a long discussion concerning Wellington's strategy in the Peninsula.

It was the sort of subject that her Mother found extremely boring.

Gina found herself wondering now who she would be able to talk to.

Who would be able to give her answers to the questions she wanted to ask about the international situation.

The newspapers were saying that the War was drawing to a close.

Napoleon was already at the end of his resources.

His disastrous invasion of Russia had made the English optimistic that the end of hostilities was in sight.

At the same time Gina thought, as her Father always had, that it was a mistake to underestimate that amazing man.

He had risen from Corporal to Emperor and

his ambition was to conquer the world.

"If only Papa were here to tell me about it all," Gina thought.

Then, because she was afraid that she was going to cry, she left the Study to go to the Library.

It was not a very large room.

It could not in any way be compared with the Library at Lavon House — their Country House.

However she saw with delight that there were some new books that she had not read before.

She thought that her Father must have bought them just before his death knowing that she would enjoy them as much as he would.

She picked them up one after the other.

Then she put them tidily back in their places.

She knew it would be a mistake to plunge immediately into a book which would stop her from thinking of anything else!

She must first be with her Mother and decide exactly what she was going to do.

"Maman first, learning afterwards," she told herself with a faint smile.

She looked at the clock and thought her Mother would be down soon.

She therefore walked down the passage to the Morning-Room.

It was there they habitually sat until luncheon-time.

After the meal was finished Gina was certain her Mother would want to go shopping.

They would drive in a carriage drawn by two

of her Father's finely bred horses.

When they returned for tea they would use the Drawing-Room.

It was all an accepted routine she had followed since she was a child.

As she sat in the window she tried to see if any new flowerbeds had been added since she had been away.

The trees certainly seemed to have grown higher and fuller.

The fountain was entrancing.

Just as it had been when she had first tried to catch in her small hands the goldfish which swam in the sculptured stone pool beneath it.

She was thinking how thrilled she had been when her Father first had it built.

Then she heard the door open.

She was just about to jump up and run towards her Mother.

Then she was aware that it was not her Mother who came into the room but a man.

He was wearing a uniform which she recognised as that of the Household Cavalry.

She thought it strange that a servant had not announced him.

He walked across the room to the grog-tray which stood in the corner beyond the fireplace.

Gina saw him pour himself out a drink from one of the cut-glass decanters.

She wondered who on earth he could be.

He took a long drink from his glass.

As he did so he threw back his head and she

was able to see him quite clearly.

He was, she realised, extremely good-looking.

In fact handsome was the right word.

He had fair hair brushed back from a square forehead, and bright blue eyes.

He obviously had no idea she was in the room.

She wondered how she should introduce herself.

He put down his glass and went to her Mother's inlaid *Secretaire*.

It stood in front of the other window.

He stood looking down at a pile of letters beside a blotter.

Then he stretched out his hand.

Gina saw him pick up a gold seal which she remembered had always stood there.

To her astonishment he put it into the pocket of his red jacket.

It was impossible to believe that he was stealing it.

At the same time she thought it was a strange thing to do.

She remembered the seal well.

Her Father had given it to her Mother as one of his presents at Christmas.

It was not only made of gold, but it had some precious stones inset on the top of it.

"I must ask him why he has taken it," Gina thought.

Then at that moment the door opened and her Mother came in.

Lady Langdale was looking very beautiful.

Her hair was arranged in a new fashion Gina had not seen before.

She was wearing one of the high-waisted gowns that were still in fashion.

They were also far more elaborate than they had been earlier in the year.

Lady Langdale's gown clung to her figure and swirled out at the bottom of the skirt.

There was a flounce of lace frills ornamented with bunches of light pink roses.

They matched the sash which encircled her small waist.

There were lace frills on her puffed sleeves and round her decolletage.

This was cut low, Gina thought, because it was what the Prince Regent admired.

The gown itself was a delicate pink which blended with the roses.

It made Lady Langdale look exceedingly glamorous.

Before Gina could rise and go to her Mother, the man who had been standing at the writing-table turned round.

"Cleo!" he exclaimed in a deep voice. "You look divine. A glorious goddess from Olympus, come to earth to bewitch poor mortals like myself!"

"I did not know you were here, Guy," Lady Langdale said. "I thought you were on guard this morning."

"I got away because I could not live another moment without seeing you," the man called

Guy replied. "Say that you too are pleased to see me, or I swear I shall blow a piece of lead through my brains."

He spoke so dramatically, in such an overtheatrical manner, that Gina thought her Mother must laugh at him.

Instead she said in a soft voice:

"You know, dear Guy, I am always pleased to see you. You have given me a very happy surprise in coming here so early."

"How could I live for another moment without seeing you?" he asked.

He took Lady Langdale's hand in his and kissed it passionately.

It was over his bent head that she saw her daughter staring at her wide-eyed.

"Oh, here you are, Dearest Gina," she said. "I thought I would find you here."

As she spoke Guy Dawes relinquished her hand, and turned to look at Gina in astonishment.

Lady Langdale put her hand on his arm.

"Now" she said, "you can meet my daughter Gina, who I told you was returning from Bath yesterday. Gina, this is Captain Guy Dawes, a friend who has been very kind to me when I have been so lonely without your Father."

Gina held out her hand.

The Captain took it in his.

As he did so, she had the unmistakable feeling that there was something wrong and she did not like him.

"So you are home from school," he said. "I

hope you will enjoy yourself amongst the bright lights of London. At the same time, because you are here, I am afraid."

"Afraid?" Lady Langdale asked. "What can make you afraid?"

"That now that you have your daughter, you will neglect me," Captain Dawes replied. "If I am no longer needed by the most beautiful, most charming woman I have ever met, the only thing I can do is to drown my despair in the Thames."

"There will be no need for you to do that," Lady Langdale said. "You must help me to find charming young men like yourself to dance with Gina and to entertain her, now that she has finished her education."

"There will be no difficulty about that," Captain Dawes replied.

Looking at Gina he spoke in what she thought was a somewhat impertinent way.

He then turned to her Mother and went on:

"She is very pretty, but how could she ever compare with Aphrodite herself? It would be impossible!"

"You are flattering me." Lady Langdale smiled.

It was, however, not a rebuke.

In fact Gina was aware that her Mother was enjoying being talked to in this exaggerated manner.

As they sat down she realised Lady Langdale was encouraging the fulsome compliments the Captain was paying her.

21

She also thought that they seemed very familiar with each other.

It seemed very strange.

Gina knew her Mother had just had her thirty-ninth birthday.

She was sure that Captain Dawes was not a day over twenty-four, if not younger.

"Why is he behaving in this extraordinary manner?" she asked herself.

Later, when he had left and she was alone with her Mother, she had asked rather tentative questions about him.

"He is such a charming young man," Lady Langdale said. "He, as you realise, adores me."

Gina did not speak and she went on:

"As you must be aware, Dearest, I have always had men in love with me. Of course I never noticed them while your Father was alive, but I have been very, very lonely since he died."

"I know that, Mama," Gina said impulsively, "and I worried about you when I was at school. You should have let me come back to be with you."

"I know, Dearest, but your Father had been very insistent that you should learn everything possible at what was the smartest school in England! So how could I be so selfish as to take you away?"

"At least I am back now," Gina said.

She hoped as she spoke that her Mother would not need Captain Dawes if she was there.

However, having done what Regimental duties

were required of him, he turned up at tea-time.

Again he walked into the room unannounced.

Gina was shocked when he came back again for dinner and she realised that he had a latchkey.

He did not have to ring for the servants to open the door.

She wanted to suggest to her Mother that it was a mistake to let anyone have a key.

Even her Mother did not use one.

But by now she had begun to realise that, if Captain Dawes was besotted by her Mother, her Mother was also extremely pleased with him.

Lady Langdale encouraged his compliments and listened to them with a smile on her lips.

She was continually patting his arm or letting him kiss her hand.

She spoke to him in a soft beguiling voice.

Gina could not remember having heard it before.

When she went up to bed she asked herself how her Mother could be so foolish as to encourage a man who was so much younger than herself.

There were several other guests for dinner.

Gina had an idea, although she might have been wrong, that they were friends of Captain Dawes rather than of her Mother.

He was in fact entertaining them at her Mother's expense.

"I must not be critical the moment I arrive," she told herself.

She lay in the darkness thinking over what had

happened during the day.

As she did so she had the uncomfortable feeling that something was wrong.

She was not certain what it was.

She just knew that Guy Dawes was putting on an act.

The things he said might have pleased her Mother, but they had not been sincere.

Once or twice she had caught what she thought was a hard look in his eyes.

She had also not forgotten the gold seal she had seen him take from her Mother's *Secretaire*.

She thought of mentioning it.

Then she told herself that it might precipitate a scene.

That was the last thing she would want when she had just come home.

"Why should he have taken it? Why?" she asked.

But there was no answer.

When Gina woke the next morning, she remembered that she and her Mother were going shopping.

"I shall be up early, Darling," her Mother had said. "We will go to Madame Rosamund's before luncheon and visit two of the other shops afterwards."

"I bought quite a lot of clothes in Bath, Mama," Gina said.

"Bath!" Lady Langdale exclaimed contemptuously. "Whatever you got there can hardly be as

24

smart as the very latest fashion in Bond Street.
Madame Rosamund is very expensive, but I want
you to shine like a star from the moment you
appear. That of course is what people will expect
from my daughter."

"I shall never be as beautiful as you, Mama."

"That is what Guy tells me," Lady Langdale
answered, "but, Dearest, you are very lovely, and
I know that a great number of men will want to
marry you."

Gina held up her hands in horror.

"You are going too quickly, Mama. I want to
meet a lot of people, to see a lot of things I had
not yet seen before going to school, and not to
think about marriage until I am much older and
the right man comes along."

"I am sure you will find the right man," her
Mother said. "Your Father married me after my
first Season. I hope you will find someone as
distinguished as he was."

Gina hesitated for a moment and then she said:

"Did you ever mind Papa being so much older
than you?"

"Oh, no!" Lady Langdale replied quickly.
"Your Father was a wonderful man, but of course
he had innumerable duties to perform and took
them very seriously. I did not fill his whole horizon as I might have done for a younger man."

Gina knew her Mother was thinking of Captain
Dawes.

After a moment she said:

"I am sure there are many men who admire

you, Mama, and it would be nice if you were friendly with some who are as important and respected as Papa was. Members of Parliament, for instance, or officials at Court."

Her Mother did not reply.

Gina knew instinctively that her Mother had no yearning for what she had just suggested.

With an intelligence which was beyond her years Gina told herself that what her Mother desired now was what she had missed in her youth.

She was therefore making up for that by listening to the nonsensical, almost ridiculous, compliments of Captain Dawes.

"I can understand what Mama is feeling," she told herself. "But why is he putting on what I am sure is an act?"

Ever since she had been a small child Gina had used her instinct.

It had told her more of the truth about people than anything she could read in books.

The girls at school teased her about it.

"Tell our fortunes, Gina," they would plead. "You know how right you were about Suzie."

Suzie had been a girl they all loved but who was terribly poor.

Her parents had scrimped and saved to be able to send her to such an expensive school.

Suzie had been absolutely frank about what she called her "poverty-stricken situation."

She had not asked for their sympathy.

She had made them laugh when she had told

them stories of how they made two ends meet.

How she often had to walk rather than spend money on a hackney-carriage.

She explained how tired her feet got.

One day when some others were having their fortunes told, Gina told Suzie's.

"Everything is going to change for the better," she said. "You will have a windfall you do not expect and it will make you very happy."

"What sort of windfall?" Suzie asked. "Is Betty going to give me one of her old gowns or something like that?"

This was a joke.

Betty, who was rich, was known to be extremely close-fisted, and would never give anyone anything.

They had all laughed, but Gina said seriously:

"No, honestly, Suzie. The sun is going to shine on you and by the end of the year you and your family will move house, and there is a marvellous time for you ahead."

"And I shall be praying that you are right," Suzie replied.

They all knew that she did not believe a word of it.

A month later Suzie had a letter from her Mother.

Her Godfather, whom she had not seen for years, had died in the West Indies where he had some property.

He had left her everything he possessed.

As he was very rich Suzie found it hard to

believe what she was reading.

"You were right, Gina! You were right! How could you have known this would happen to me?"

After that Gina had difficulty in keeping the girls from consulting her day and night.

"I will only do you once every two months," she said finally, "so it is no use asking me in between."

It was not only fortunes at which she was so perceptive.

She knew what a person was thinking.

To herself, she admitted that everyone had vibrations which told her whether they were good or bad.

Not that she had met any really bad people.

Just those who she knew were insincere and said one thing meaning another.

She knew what they actually meant.

She was therefore quite sure that Captain Dawes had some ulterior motive for the way he was behaving with her Mother.

He may admire Mama, she told herself, but he is not in love with her as he pretends to be.

Why should he be, when she is so much older?

She remembered that her Father had been older than her Mother, but that was a different thing.

There was no doubt that he loved her.

He wanted to protect her from any unhappiness she might feel from the people in the world in which they lived.

"Women can be very unkind to a woman who

is more beautiful than they are," he had said once to Gina. "Your Mother is so trusting. She believes everything she is told. I am always afraid that one day she will be bitterly hurt when she is deceived."

"She will be safe as long as she is with us, Papa," Gina had said.

Lord Langdale had put his arm round his daughter.

"You are a very wise and sensible girl, my precious Daughter. If you use your brain you will survive any difficulty, whatever it may be."

Gina knew he was thinking that her Mother did not use her brain where people were concerned.

Gina wondered now how she could warn her against Captain Dawes without upsetting her.

"I must talk to Mama," she decided.

But she knew it would be difficult in the daytime.

They were driving in the open carriage through the streets.

Her Mother was always seeing acquaintances to whom she waved.

So far since she had come home there had hardly been a moment when there were not people calling.

Or when Captain Dawes was not sitting and looking at her Mother in what he believed was an adoring attitude.

She remembered her Mother had not come up to bed when she had.

She had remained downstairs with two other guests besides Captain Dawes.

He had suggested that they have a game of whist.

That had given Gina the opportunity to slip away as she was not wanted.

She would go to bed as she was still tired after her journey.

The roads had been bad in some parts.

Although the carriage was well-sprung, she still felt bruised from rolling over a number of boulders.

Finding she could not sleep, she thought she would go and talk to her Mother as she had done as a child.

If her Father was late at the House of Lords, she would sit on her Mother's bed.

They would talk until they were both sleepy, or her Father returned home.

Gina got out of bed.

She put on a pretty dressing-gown she had bought in Bath. It was of blue satin and very becoming.

Then she crossed the passage from her room to her Mother's.

She opened the door quietly in case her Mother was asleep.

By the light of the candle burning beside the bed she saw to her surprise that her Mother was not there.

She was certain that she had heard her come upstairs.

Then Gina thought that she must be in the Boudoir which opened out of the bedroom.

Gina crossed to the communicating door.

As she reached it she heard voices, and stopped still.

Someone was with her Mother in the Boudoir.

She knew who it was — Captain Dawes.

The door was ajar and she heard her Mother say:

"Of course I understand. I know, dear Guy, it is very difficult for a young man not to get into debt under those circumstances."

"I am desperate," Guy Dawes said in a dramatic manner, "simply because my debt of £500 is one of honour. You know, my perfect goddess, my beautiful Aphrodite, that I must honour it."

"Of course you must," Lady Langdale agreed, "and you will find a Banker's Order in the drawer."

"You are kindness itself. You are an Angel sent to me from Heaven. How can I thank you?" Captain Dawes asked passionately.

Listening, Gina was aware that he was kissing her Mother's hand.

Now she thought she knew the reason for his attentions.

She heard him go to the drawer and open it.

"I have found it," he said.

"Fill it in for me," Lady Langdale told him, "and I will sign it."

There was the sound of a chair being pulled out.

Then a few seconds ticked by until Captain

Dawes suddenly exclaimed:

"Oh My God! I have made a mistake!"

"What have you done?" Lady Langdale enquired.

"You must forgive me for being so stupid. I was thinking of my debts and the desperate plight I am in. I have made this order out for £1,000 instead of £500. Forgive me, forgive me! I will tear it up."

"Of course not," Lady Langdale replied. "If you have other debts you should have told me."

"How can I impose on anyone so beautiful? Anyone so kind and compassionate as yourself?" Guy Dawes asked. "I am ashamed. Horrified at myself for being so foolish. But only you understand."

"Of course I understand," Lady Langdale said. "Give me the Order and let me sign it."

Gina had heard enough.

Very quietly she withdrew from the bedroom, closing the door behind her.

She went back to her own room and got into bed.

Now she was aware what Guy Dawes was up to.

He was not only conning her Mother into giving him £1,000, he had also stolen the gold seal from the desk downstairs.

There might be dozens of other things he had taken from the house without her Mother, who was always somewhat vague, being aware of it.

Gina felt her anger rising.

"How dare he impose on Mama in this manner," she raged, "just because Papa is not here to protect her from men like him?"

Then she wondered almost desperately what she could do.

She knew it would be no use talking to her Mother.

She would not believe that Captain Dawes was just using her for his own selfish needs.

"I must talk to someone. Someone who will help me," she told herself.

But she could not think who that could be!

chapter two

Gina slept badly and kept waking up worrying over her mother and Captain Guy Dawes.

When morning came she went down to breakfast, knowing her Mother had hers in her own room.

She therefore ate alone.

When she had finished, she thought she would look round the house to see if anything else was missing.

She went first to her Father's Study.

As she might have expected the books were all still there and, as far as she could remember, nothing had been removed from his desk.

Then a thought suddenly struck her.

She went to the Drawing-Room to look at his collection of snuff-boxes.

They were displayed in glass cases on the top of inlaid tables.

As a child she had been fascinated by the beauty of the enamel and the precious stones which surrounded some of the miniatures.

Gina approached the table which contained the most valuable of his collection — there was another table at the other end of the room.

She was praying she might be mistaken.

She was certain her Mother would not have noticed if any of the snuff-boxes were missing.

She had never shown any particular interest in the collection.

At first glance she thought the snuff-boxes were all there.

Then she remembered one which had a miniature of Catherine the Great on the lid.

It was surrounded by a circle of diamonds, and both diamonds and pearls decorated the rest of the box.

"It is reputed to have been given to Catherine the Great by Prince Orlov," her father had told her, "at the same time that he presented her with the famous 'Orlov Diamond,' which is one of the most spectacular in the whole world."

It was also, Gina remembered, reputed to be very unlucky.

Its future history had proved that to be the truth.

She saw now that the Catherine the Great snuff-box was missing and also two other boxes she remembered distinctly.

One of them, which went back to the sixteenth century, depicted an unknown soldier who was very handsome.

The other was one she had loved because it was decorated with flowers.

They were inset with tiny precious stones the same colour as the petals.

To make sure she had not made a mistake

Gina ran to the other end of the Drawing-Room where the other table stood.

The snuff-boxes on that table were more amusing than those she had just been looking at.

One was shaped like a ship, another a pip, and a third was in the form of a King Charles Spaniel.

The last was missing.

There was no sign of the three boxes which had stood on the other table.

For a moment Gina was furious.

She felt like going upstairs and denouncing Captain Dawes to her Mother.

She also thought she might have him taken before the Magistrates and sent to prison.

Then it was as if her Father was talking to her, telling her not to panic and to keep calm.

She knew that such actions would cause a terrible scene.

Moreover her Mother would probably not listen to her.

Gina had watched her last night listening to Captain Dawes's compliments and enjoying every word of what he said.

'If I accuse him, Mama will only stand up in his defence,' she thought. 'But she would also be hurt and distressed, and that is something Papa would never have allowed.'

Once again the question was back in her mind as to what she should do.

How could she prevent Captain Dawes from stealing more treasures and taking more money from her Mother?

'The first thing,' she thought, 'was to lock up everything of value that she could.'

There was a gold key in the locks of both cases, and she turned them and put the keys in her pocket.

Then she thought of going round the house to see what else was missing.

She was wondering if Guy Dawes had already got his hands on some of her Mother's jewellery.

Her Father, because he adored his wife, used to give her magnificent gifts of jewellery at Christmas and on her birthday.

He always gave her jewellery because he knew she preferred that to anything else.

"I thought once of giving your Mother a very pretty picture by Fragonard," he said once to Gina, "because the woman he depicted was so very like her. But I knew she would rather have a diamond necklace."

"She has one already, Papa!" Gina exclaimed.

"I have found from long experience," her Father replied, "that beautiful women can never have too many jewels to enhance their beauty."

He smiled before he went on:

"When you get a little older you must tell me which precious stone is your favourite."

"I would rather have a book, Papa," Gina replied.

Her Father laughed.

"I doubt if you will say that when you are eighteen, my Dearest," he replied, "but as far as I am concerned, you can have both!"

'I am eighteen and I do not want precious gems,' Gina now thought defiantly, 'but I hate the idea of Captain Dawes getting his dirty fingers on Mama's jewels.'

When her Mother came downstairs she had control of herself.

She kissed her affectionately, thinking how lovely she looked.

She thought it was not surprising that her Father had wanted to protect her.

"We are going shopping, Dearest," Lady Langdale said. "Are you ready?"

"I have only to put on my bonnet," Gina answered, "and I hope it is one of which you approve."

It was a very pretty bonnet trimmed with wildflowers and with ribbons which tied under Gina's small pointed chin.

Lady Langdale looked at it for a few seconds before she said:

"Yes, it suits you. At the same time I am sure we can find an even more attractive one at the Milliner I always patronise."

"Before we go there," Gina said, "I would like, Mama, to stop at the Bank. Now that I am home I want to arrange that I can pay my own bills."

She gave a little sigh before she finished:

"You remember it was Papa who always paid them in the past."

"Just as he paid mine," Lady Langdale said.

There was just a suspicion of a wistful note in her voice which Gina thought was encouraging.

If she was missing her husband, perhaps she would not be so enraptured by Captain Dawes.

However, as they drove on, Lady Langdale kept speaking of him in one context or another.

"Captain Dawes is a magnificent dancer," she said, "and there was a wonderful Ball at Carlton House last week. I only wish you could have been there. The loveliest women in London were present but Guy told me I eclipsed them all, and I like to think he was right."

"Of course he was, Mama," Gina said, "but surely, there were a great number of other gentlemen longing to dance with you?"

"Quite a few," Lady Langdale admitted, "but Guy is very possessive and gets so jealous if I dance with other men rather than him."

Gina drew in her breath.

Then she said:

"Perhaps, Mama, it is a mistake for you to be gossiped about by those spiteful women. They will undoubtedly do so if you dance too often with one man."

Lady Langdale shrugged her shoulders.

"Why should I worry about them, Dearest? They are only jealous."

Gina thought it a mistake to say any more.

The horses drew up outside Coutts Bank.

As they did so her Mother said:

"I will not come in with you. I thought the Manager last week was somewhat impertinent, saying I was spending too much money. I do not consider it is *his* business!"

"Then you stay here, Mama. I will not be very long," Gina said.

She went into the Bank and was shown immediately into the Manager's private room.

She had met him before as her Father had banked with Coutts all his life.

The Manager, Mr. Matthews, held out his hand, greeting her enthusiastically.

"It is delightful to see you, Miss Lang," he said. "I was thinking you would be coming home soon from your school in Bath."

"I am glad to be home," Gina said, "and I have come at once to see what arrangements can be made for me to draw cheques and pay my own bills, which is what I know Papa would have wanted."

"Your Father told me not long before his death," Mr. Matthews replied, "that as you were an extremely intelligent young woman, he wanted you to have control of your own affairs as soon as you were grown up."

He sighed before he went on:

"Of course, His Lordship had no idea at that time that he was likely to die so soon. He did however make it very clear to me, and of course it was in his Will, that you should be 'your own master,' so to speak."

"That is what I want to be," Gina answered.

Mr. Matthews smiled.

"It is very unusual for a young lady, or for an older woman for that matter, to control her own money, but owing to this dreadful War there are now a great many widows who have to look after themselves."

"I only hope they are capable of doing so," Gina said. "My Mother told me that you were warning her last week that she was being too extravagant."

For a moment the Manager was silent. Then he said:

"I had of course, Miss Lang, no intention of discussing Her Ladyship's private affairs with you, but as you have brought up the subject, I must tell you that I am a little perturbed at the way Lady Langdale is spending more than she ever did in your Father's time."

Gina was listening intently.

Then she said a little tentatively:

"Entirely confidentially, Mr. Matthews, as I know my Father trusted and confided in you, I want to ask you if my Mother has been giving large sums of money to a certain Captain Guy Dawes?"

Mr. Matthews looked startled.

"I am surprised you should know this," he replied. "But of course, if your mother has confided in you, then I can only say that I consider the amount that Captain Dawes has received is out of all proportion to her allowance."

Gina was aware that her Father in his Will had left her everything he possessed, with the exception of a very large allowance to her Mother.

Lady Langdale had the right to live in either of his houses for as long as she lived.

Thinking it would be a mistake to seem too curious she said:

"Thank you, Mr. Matthews, for being frank with me. I will do what I can about Mama's extravagance, but you know as well as I do that Papa gave her everything she wanted, and she never had to handle money herself."

"I am aware of that," Mr. Matthews said, "and I think it would be wise, Miss Lang, if you could tactfully hint to your Mother that she is falling into debt."

"I will do that," Gina replied.

She then received Banker's Drafts and the Notes of Hand that she required.

Thanking Mr. Matthews again she left the Bank.

It was difficult because she was so worried to show a really concentrated interest in the bonnets which her Mother made her buy.

Or the gowns which they inspected in another shop.

Then it was nearly time to return home for luncheon.

Lady Langdale however said she would like to drive down Rotten Row to see who was riding this morning.

When they reached Rotten Row there was still a number of open carriages there like their own.

Exquisitely dressed women were driving in each of them, holding small sunshades over their heads.

Lady Langdale seemed to know them all.

There were also some very smart ladies riding on outstandingly well-bred horses, which made Gina envious.

She had ridden in London with her father.

But she had never thought it was very amusing compared to being able to gallop over the fields at Lavon.

Now she thought that if her Mother insisted on staying in London she would have to ride in the Park just for exercise.

Lady Langdale stopped her carriage to talk to two friends to whom she introduced Gina.

Then as it grew later the carriages and horses began to disperse.

"We had better return home," Lady Langdale said, "and to-morrow, we must come earlier. I had forgotten that I should introduce you to those of my friends who come here every morning."

"That would be delightful, Mama!" Gina agreed.

The horses turned round and were making for Stanhope Gate when Lady Langdale exclaimed:

"Oh, there is the Marquis of Mortlake! He is the most handsome man in London! Your Father knew him and had a high opinion of him as a most promising young man. He was in the Life Guards, so Guy has often spoken of him."

Gina saw a very handsome man riding an enormous black stallion.

He looked so much a part of his horse that she knew he must be an outstanding rider.

When they passed him he raised his top-hat politely to her Mother.

As he did so Gina felt as though a voice told her that the Marquis could help her.

If he had known her father, and also knew Captain Dawes, then it would not be difficult to beg for his assistance.

As they drove on she felt as if her prayers had been answered.

As they drove back to Berkeley Square she was planning what she must do.

After luncheon Lady Langdale said she wanted to lie down.

"We are going to dine to-night with the Countess of Dudley," she said. "Guy will also be there and I want to look my best, otherwise he might be disappointed."

"Of course you must, Mama!" Gina agreed. "I am sure you have a beautiful gown to wear."

"I think you will admire it," Lady Langdale replied. "And if Guy comes in after tea, I will ask him to choose which of my jewels should go with it."

With difficulty Gina prevented herself from screaming at the idea.

If Captain Dawes was going to handle her Mother's jewels, she was quite certain that some of them would disappear.

"As Papa always used to help you," she said, "I hope, Mama, you will let me take his place. It is something I would love to do."

Lady Langdale looked surprised. Then she said:

"Of course, Dearest, if that is what you want,

and I am sure you have very good taste. I must glitter, but not, as your father would say, 'go over the top' as that would be vulgar."

"Of course it would, Mama, and so we will consider all your lovely jewels and decide which of them will best frame your beauty."

She nearly added:

"Just as the diamonds framed Catherine the Great before the snuff-box was stolen."

Then she told herself that she must not upset her Mother. To do so would be very unkind.

Whatever else he might do, Captain Dawes was making her happy.

However it was very unfortunate that she should choose a thief as a companion.

As soon as her Mother had gone up to rest, Gina ordered a carriage.

She also told the Butler she wanted one of the housemaids to accompany her.

"We are making only a short journey," she said, "as I believe the Marquis of Mortlake lives quite near."

"At Mortlake House in Park Lane, Miss Gina," the Butler replied.

"That is what I thought," Gina replied.

The carriage took only a little over five minutes to carry her from Berkeley Square to a very large mansion half-way down Park Lane.

There was an in-and-out drive in front of the house.

Gina guessed there was a large garden behind it.

The portico, like the house itself, was very imposing.

The footman got down from the box.

Gina told him to ask if the Marquis would see Miss Gina Lang on a matter of urgency.

The footman relayed her message to the Butler who answered the door.

There was a long wait before he returned to say: "His Lordship'll see Miss Lang, but he has 'nother appointment in a short while."

Gina thought with a faint smile that she had heard this reply before.

It was when her Father wished to give importunate callers as little time as possible.

Thinking she should be grateful for small mercies, she hurriedly stepped down from the carriage.

The Marquis of Mortlake had luncheon with one of his closest friends, Harry Vivian.

They had served in the same Regiment until he was invalided out of the Army.

Harry was home on compassionate leave as his Mother had just died.

The Marquis was intent on hearing everything that was happening in Spain.

"I miss you, oh, God, how I miss you all!" he exclaimed.

"You are lucky to be out of the war," Harry remarked. "Wellington is confident we shall win. At the same time, those damned French have a hell of a lot of fight left in them."

"It is extraordinary," the Marquis said, "that here in London nobody seems to worry about the war. The Prince Regent is giving extravagant parties night after night, and naturally the whole of the *Beau Monde* follows his lead."

"I forgot to ask you — is your shoulder better?"

The Marquis had been shot in the shoulder, which was the reason why he had been sent home over two years ago.

Almost immediately after his return he had inherited his title.

He had tried in every way he could to be allowed to return to the Peninsula and his Regiment.

However the Prince Regent as well as the War Office had refused.

"For one thing, I do not want to lose you to a French bullet," the Prince Regent had said, "and the second reason is that, if you were taken prisoner, the French would make such a coup of it that it would be bad for the morale of the troops."

In fact the wound in the Marquis's shoulder had taken a long time to heal.

He knew there was a certain amount of sense in the War Office's decision.

They assured him that he had done everything he could and would be of more use at home than abroad.

He was kept in constant touch with what was going on.

This was because the Generals in the War

Office needed his help and valued his advice.

He was able to explain to them the difficulties that Wellington was encountering in the territory in which he was fighting.

Harry had been even more blunt about his staying at home.

"You have already won two gold medals for gallantry," he said. "Stop being greedy and wanting a third!"

The Marquis smiled a little ruefully.

"I have no wish to be gallant," he replied. "All I want is to fight side by side with the men I know and trust and who have always been prepared to follow me and obey my orders."

"They adore you, as you well know," Harry said, "although God knows why!"

He was teasing the Marquis as he had always done since they were boys at school.

Harry understood better than anybody else how frustrated his friend was feeling at being invalided out of the Army.

Especially when the hope of victory was on the horizon.

To change the subject he said:

"A little bird tells me that you have a new 'Charmer' in your life. Do I know her?"

The Marquis smiled and answered:

"I do not think you have met her, but her name is Imogen Strangway."

"Do you mean the Duke of Milchester's daughter?" Harry asked. "I have certainly heard of her!"

The Marquis grinned.

"Most men have!"

"She certainly has a reputation!" Harry added.

The Marquis knew exactly what his friend meant.

Lady Imogen was without doubt one of the most alluring, exotic, passionate women he had ever met.

Because he was so handsome, the Marquis had been pursued from the moment he left Eton.

Before he had been sent abroad he had indulged in a number of *affaires de coeur*.

They had kept the gossips' tongues wagging.

Imogen however had come into his life only two months ago.

She was certainly different from any other woman to whom he had made love.

He did not doubt that she had manoeuvred him into the situation that now existed between them.

She had done it with a cleverness he could only admire.

Harry said now:

"I must meet *la Femme Fatale.*"

"As you will be spending every spare moment of your leave with me, you will meet her tomorrow."

"At a party — or here?" Harry asked.

"Here," the Marquis answered. "I much prefer my own food and my own wine. I will let Imogen choose the guests. They will be immaterial to the main roles in the Play."

Harry had a slight frown between his eyes.

"You are not thinking of marrying her, are you?"

"Good Lord, no!" the Marquis replied quickly. "I have no intention of marrying anyone. But Imogen does keep me from thinking too bitterly of what I am missing abroad."

"What you are missing is a great deal of abject discomfort," Harry said, "as well as a lack of edible food, and the continual worry as to whether the ammunition will arrive for which the men are waiting."

He saw the twinkle in the Marquis's eyes and went on:

"Or, on the other hand, if you have the ammunition, whether there will be any sign of the men who have to use it!"

The Marquis laughed.

"That is a very good description of what seems to happen every day on a battlefield."

"Nothing has changed," Harry said, "except that the discomfort is even worse where we are at the moment, and there is nothing to offset the lack of good horses and the asinine orders of most of the Commanders."

The Marquis laughed again.

"Poor Harry! You had better extend your leave for as long as you can."

"I certainly intend to enjoy every second of it. So I hope you are going to provide me with something warm and attractive to-morrow evening."

"I will tell Imogen what you require," the Marquis said. "I am sure she will not disappoint you."

Harry was quiet for a minute or so. Then he said:

"From what I have heard of Lady Imogen in the past and what I have learnt already since my return, I am sure you should be careful not to find yourself trapped."

"You mean she is trying to marry me," the Marquis said with a cynical note in his voice. "My dear Harry, that is nothing new. Every mother of a marriageable daughter, every widow who is looking for a new husband to support her, has tried to catch me in one way or another. You know as well as I do that I am a confirmed bachelor, and that is how I intend to remain."

"I agree with you because I feel the same," Harry said. "However, I have been told over and over again that Lady Imogen always gets her own way in the end."

"Then, I assure you, she will be disappointed this time," the Marquis said.

Looking at the Marquis, Harry thought he could understand that even apart from his title and his money women would desire him.

He noticed however since he had been home that there was a cynical look about his friend which had not been there before.

He knew already that the Marquis was shocked at how lightly the Social World was treating the war.

It was impossible to explain it to men who had

51

never heard a shot fired in anger.

Or to make the Bucks and Beaux who drank and gambled in the Clubs of St. James's interested in what was happening abroad.

Harry was not exaggerating when he described their sufferings.

They grew worse and worse as they advanced farther from Portugal into Spain, fighting every inch of the way.

There were long periods when they waited for provisions to come up from the Base.

The Officers, like their men, were often extremely hungry until the supplies arrived.

There were desperate moments when, as Harry had said, they were short of ammunition.

They would have no idea where, or even whether, it would arrive at all.

There was the constant fear of spies amongst the local people through whose territory they were operating.

Then there was the constant difficulty of getting the wounded treated and taken to safety

No one knew better than Harry how magnificent the Marquis had been.

How well-deserved were his medals for gallantry.

He had seemed untiring.

It was his high spirits that had kept his men not only alert, but also laughing.

He could turn the most desperate situation into a joke.

Harry knew that every man under his command would have laid down his life for him.

But this new mood of cynicism was something he had never encountered in his friend before.

"I hear," he said, "that you are doing an excellent job at the War Office and they are very grateful to you."

"I do not know who told you that nonsense," the Marquis replied. "They ask me a lot of damned silly questions, to most of which it is quite impossible to find an answer."

"What about spies?" Harry asked. "Out there we think London is crawling with them."

"If it is, they disguise themselves very well," the Marquis answered. "There was one man who somehow got into the Foreign Office as a Clerk, but he was soon disposed of."

"Quite seriously," Harry said, "my father, who is a great friend of the Foreign Secretary, tells me that Viscount Castlereagh is worried."

He dropped his voice as he continued:

"Information regarding the movement of troops and many other important matters is being relayed in one way or another to Napoleon."

"If I have heard that story once, I have heard it a thousand times," the Marquis said. "Personally I do not believe that Napoleon has that many spies amongst us, and, if he has, you and I are not likely to meet them."

"They would not have to be French," Harry argued.

"If you think I am going to suspect that every Englishman who asks me about my Regiment is a spy, you are barking up the wrong tree!" the Marquis said. "I have never believed that the French espionage is anything but a lot of talk to frighten fat old Generals who do not have enough to do!"

"Very well," Harry said. "I am only telling you what they think on the Peninsula. I am inclined to believe it because I think Napoleon is getting desperate. The last lot of prisoners we took were mostly boys under seventeen."

"That is interesting," the Marquis remarked in a different tone of voice. "Do you really mean he is running short of men?"

"His casualties have been enormous," Harry replied, "but somehow, by sheer will-power, black magic, call it what you will, he manages to go on fighting."

"I think you had better come with me to-morrow to the War Office," the Marquis said in a businesslike tone. "It was stupid of me not to think of it before, but your help could be invaluable."

"All right," Harry agreed, "although I have nothing to tell of any particular interest."

"Think hard," the Marquis ordered. "We are always thrilled when the unexpected turns up."

"Just as in private life," Harry said pointedly.

"Which is not often enough," the Marquis retorted.

The Butler came to the Marquis's side.

"Excuse me, M'Lord, but there's a young lady outside, a Miss Gina Lang, who says she wishes t' speak t' Your Lordship on an urgent matter."

"Ah-ha!" Harry exclaimed, "an urgent young lady certainly sounds interesting!"

"I am quite sure it is either a request for money for a Church that is falling down," the Marquis replied, "or else some Charity of which I have never heard whose finances are on the rocks."

"I seem to know the name 'Lang,' " Harry said thoughtfully, "but I cannot put a face to it."

"Th' young lady's come in a smart carriage, M'Lord," the Butler interrupted helpfully, "with a coachman an' a footman on th' box."

Harry laughed.

"That certainly does not denote a request to save ragged boys or help pregnant women in distress!"

The Marquis sighed.

"I suppose I ought to see her," he said, "but tell her, Dawkins, that I can only spare her a few minutes and that I have a previous appointment which I cannot miss."

Dawkins, who was an old servant and had known the Marquis since he was a small boy, nodded.

"Leave it t' me, M'Lord."

"Do you have a lot of women ringing the bell wanting to see you?" Harry asked when they were alone.

"Not so many strangers," the Marquis said, "and they are usually inside before I can stop them."

"That is nothing new," Harry replied. "Do you

remember that girl in Oxford we could never get rid of? What was her name?"

"I know who you mean," the Marquis said. "Quite a pretty girl, but she would never take 'no' for an answer."

"I suppose that might be the story of your life," Harry quipped.

The Marquis rose from the table.

"Come and help me talk to Miss Lang," he said. "I will take a bet with you that it is some Charity or other."

"I think you will find it concerns yourself," Harry replied.

"Done!" the Marquis said. "Now come and watch me listen to a pitiful tale of those in need."

"I shall do nothing of the sort!" Harry replied. "I will sit in your Study and read the newspapers, but do not be too long or I may fall asleep."

"I must say, you are of very little help in an emergency," the Marquis retorted.

They walked from the Dining-Room side by side.

Dawkins was waiting at the door of the small Drawing-Room which was on the Ground Floor.

Harry quickly passed him and disappeared into the Marquis's Study.

For a moment the Marquis thought he was a fool to waste his time.

He contemplated telling Dawkins to send Miss Lang away.

Then as if he remembered it was his duty, if a very boring one, he waited for Dawkins to open the door.

chapter three

In the Drawing-Room after the Butler had left her, Gina suddenly felt a sense of panic sweep over her.

In her anxiety to help her Mother she had not really thought of what the Marquis's reaction might be to her request.

Now that she was in his house she realised that he might be entirely indifferent to her troubles.

Worse still, he might laugh at them.

She had heard about him as a hero of the war and a very distinguished personage

This had blinded her to the fact that he was a young man who had been involved in a series of love-affairs.

Until now she had paid no attention to this.

When she had seen him in the Park she had thought only that he had known her Father.

He had also been in the same Regiment as Guy Dawes.

She had felt that he would understand her problem.

Now she thought she had made a mistake.

It was something she must cope with herself

without asking for a stranger's help.

She had an urgent desire to leave the house, get back into the carriage and go home.

'I could say I have changed my mind,' she thought, 'or perhaps that I feel ill.'

The whole idea of coming here to talk to a stranger about her family's private affairs was absurd.

'How can I possibly tell a man I have never met before,' Gina asked herself, 'that my Mother is infatuated with a man who is young enough to be her son?'

Even worse than what she already feared, the Marquis might talk about what she told him.

That would create the very scandal she was trying to avoid.

'How can I have been so foolish,' she wondered, 'as to come here without considering every aspect of it? I must go . . . I know I must . . . go!'

She got up from the chair on which she had been sitting and started to walk towards the door.

She had almost reached it when it opened and the Marquis came in.

Gina stood still and he looked at her in surprise.

She was certainly not the 'Do-gooder' he had expected her to be.

They were usually middle-aged or very plain women.

Facing him was one of the prettiest girls, for she seemed little more, he had ever seen.

He was aware that as he came into the room she had been about to leave it.

He looked at her more closely and realised that she was frightened.

It was a look he had seen often enough in Portugal.

It was obvious in the faces of the women who were fleeing either from the French or the English soldiers.

He had however never seen it in the eyes of a Lady of Quality, which undoubtedly his visitor was.

There was silence until the Marquis said:

"I think you wanted to see me."

He spoke in a quiet, calm way.

It was the voice he used when he was interviewing a young soldier who had run away at the first sound of gunfire.

There was a perceptible pause before Gina managed to reply:

"I . . . I have . . . changed my . . . mind and think it a . . . mistake to . . . bother you."

The words came from her lips a little incoherently.

The Marquis, still in his quiet way, replied:

"You are making me curious, Miss Lang, and as you said you wished to see me urgently, I feel it would be a waste of your time if you now run away."

"But you . . . you are busy," Gina stammered, "and have . . . more important . . . matters to . . . concern you."

The Marquis smiled.

"That is for me to decide."

As he spoke he was aware that his visitor was still intent upon leaving him.

It made him even more curious.

"Now suppose we sit down," he suggested, "and you tell me why you came to see me and how I can help you?"

He saw she was still indecisive and added:

"I promise, if it is humanly possible, I will do so.

Gina's eyes seemed to light up.

For a moment the frightened look disappeared.

"Do you mean it?" she asked.

"I never say what I do not mean," the Marquis answered.

As he spoke he walked towards the fireplace.

As if Gina could no longer gainsay him she followed.

The Marquis indicated the sofa and she sat down on the edge of it.

She clasped her hands in her lap, and he had the idea that she was forcing herself to think calmly.

Gina herself had a gift of intuition about people.

But the Marquis also had developed over the years an almost clairvoyant ability to find out the truth about the men he commanded.

It had made him one of the most outstanding Officers in Wellington's Army.

The soldiers themselves spoke of him as a wizard.

"It ain't no use hidin' anyfing from 'Engis," they used to say. " 'E forces it outa yer afore ye knows wot's 'appenin'."

That they referred to him by his Christian name was a compliment they paid only to one other Officer.

That was Wellington himself.

The men called him 'Arfur,' or 'Artie,' and they worshipped the ground he walked on.

The Marquis knew now without being told that Gina was not only very young but very vulnerable.

He knew too that she was deeply perturbed by something.

At the same time she was regretting having approached him for some reason he did not understand.

Because he felt it would relieve the tension he sat down in the nearest armchair to the sofa.

Crossing his legs he appeared to be completely at his ease.

"Now, tell me, Miss Lang," he said, "why you have called to see me. Shall I say, in case it is worrying you, that anything you tell me will be entirely confidential."

Because that was what was specially worrying her, Gina thought it was extraordinary that he should know what was in her mind.

It made everything easier.

"Thank you," she said. "I . . . I had not thought, until I came . . . here that I was being . . . indiscreet about somebody other than . . .

61

myself. It would . . . damage the person . . . considerably if what I have to . . . say went . . . outside this room."

"You have my word that it will go no further," the Marquis answered.

He saw that she was still finding it difficult to know how to start and he therefore said:

"Your name is Lang. Are you any relation to the beautiful Lady Langdale whom I have met at many parties?"

"Sh-she is my . . . Mother," Gina replied.

"Your Mother?" the Marquis exclaimed. "Then of course I knew your Father and admired him tremendously. You must miss him very much."

"More than I can . . . ever say," Gina replied in a low voice. "And now that I have . . . returned from . . . School it has been . . . agonising not to . . . find him at home."

"You have just come from School?" the Marquis asked.

"Papa sent me to a Finishing School in Bath. I have been there for nearly two years. As you can understand, it was a long way to come home, even for the holidays."

The Marquis understood why she looked so young.

Also why she seemed not to have the self-assurance of the Ladies he met in the Social World.

"Now you are home for good," he prompted, "but there is something upsetting you which brought you here to ask my advice."

"That . . . is right," Gina said. "But it was while I was waiting for . . . you just now that I . . . realised that it was not only an . . . impertinence . . . but also . . . an indiscretion, and . . . that was why I was . . . leaving."

"Then shall I say before we go any further," the Marquis said, "that I will be not only willing to help your Father's daughter, but also proud to do so."

Gina drew in her breath.

"That is what I . . . hoped perhaps . . . you would feel . . . before I came here."

"You thought of approaching me?" the Marquis asked. "Why me?"

Without thinking Gina told the truth.

"When I saw you riding in the Park this morning I suddenly . . . felt that you were the . . . one person I could . . . turn to. It was as if . . . Papa was . . . telling me to come . . . to you."

Even as she spoke she felt it a very strange thing to say to somebody she had never met before.

She was usually extremely discreet about her personal feelings where anything other than what was perfectly normal was concerned.

She had told the fortunes of the girls at School.

Yet when she used her instinct where she herself was concerned, she never talked about it.

"Well, now that you are here," the Marquis said, "I am waiting for you to tell me what is wrong."

Because he seemed so sympathetic, Gina, without looking at him, said:

"It concerns . . . Captain Guy Dawes . . . who is in your . . . Regiment . . . which of course . . . many years ago . . . was also Papa's."

"I know of Captain Dawes," the Marquis said. "I have seen him at several parties I have attended. Is he making advances to you?"

He thought as he spoke that as she had only just come home from School it was unlikely.

In any case, from what he remembered hearing of Dawes, he preferred the company of older women.

"N-no . . . I have only . . . just met . . . him," Gina replied, "but . . . he is . . . ingratiating himself with . . . my Mother . . . and is . . . taking a great deal of . . . money from her."

The Marquis sat up.

For a moment he did not speak. Then he asked:

"When you say 'a great deal of money,' what do you mean, Miss Lang?"

"The Bank has warned Mama that she is spending the allowance which my Father left her in his Will too extravagantly. Also I ascertained that Captain Dawes has obtained large sums from her."

"It seems extraordinary to me, seeing how young Dawes is," the Marquis remarked, "that your Mother should allow him to persuade her into giving him sums of any consequence."

"I went to Mama's room to talk to her," Gina said in a low voice, "and she was in her . . .

Boudoir with Captain Dawes. I overheard . . ."

Gina stopped for a moment thinking it sounded appalling for her to have eavesdropped on their conversation.

Then she went on:

"I . . . I heard her . . . agree to give Captain Dawes the sum of five-hundred pounds to settle . . . a debt of Honour, but he wrote out a Banker's Draft for . . . a thousand pounds . . . by mistake, as he said, and Mama told him not to . . . alter it."

"I can understand that you were shocked by this," the Marquis said. "Did you speak to your Mother about such generosity?"

Gina shook her head.

"I knew it would . . . upset her. She has never . . . understood money because Papa . . . always handled it for her. But that is not the only . . . reason why I . . . came to you."

"What else?" the Marquis asked.

"I was in the Morning-Room when Captain Dawes arrived, and he did not know I was there," Gina related. "I saw him take a golden seal, which my Father had given to my Mother, from the writing-table and put it in his pocket."

"Are you sure about this?" the Marquis asked sharply. "You realise, Miss Lang, it is a very serious accusation to make about an Officer in the Household Cavalry?"

"I . . . I thought there . . . must be some . . . explanation," Gina answered, "but when I looked at Papa's collection of . . . snuff-boxes which are very . . . valuable, I found that . . . three of the . . . best were missing from one table where they were displayed, and the most . . . valuable one from another."

The Marquis got to his feet.

This was certainly something far more serious than he had expected.

"I suppose there is no way of proving that it was Captain Dawes who took the snuff-boxes?" he asked slowly.

"I would not have . . . imagined it could be . . . him," Gina replied, "had I not . . . seen him take the . . . gold seal from the writing-table. Perhaps there are . . . other things missing from the house . . . but I have not had a . . . chance to look at . . . everything."

"You have not spoken to your Mother about all this?"

"Papa always protected Mama from being hurt or upset . . . and, in fact, I do not think she would . . . believe me," Gina replied.

"Very likely not," the Marquis agreed.

"But you do . . . understand . . . I do not know what to do . . . and I am . . . afraid he may take . . . some of Mama's jewellery . . . or anything else that is in . . . the house."

"If he did so, surely Lady Langdale would be aware of it?" the Marquis asked.

"She has not noticed the snuff-boxes," Gina replied, "but I think she would . . . notice any . . . jewellery, of which she is . . . very fond."

She looked up at the Marquis piteously saying:

"If she accused him there would be a terrible scandal. That would be very bad for . . . her and would, I know, have distressed Papa."

"I realise that too," the Marquis said, "and I can understand your dilemma, which I agree is very worrying."

"What shall . . . I do? What . . . can I do?" Gina asked. "If I let things go on as they are, Captain Dawes will take more and more of . . . Mama's money, and steal the treasures which Papa . . . left and which now really . . . belong to me."

The Marquis put his fingers up to his forehead.

He was thinking that this was an extraordinary problem such as he had little expected to be brought to him.

Yet which he felt honour-bound to solve one way or another.

It involved the late Lord Langdale, who had been a highly respected and honourable Statesman.

It would also create a scandal around his beautiful wife who was *persona grata* at Carlton House.

The Marquis had to think also of his Regiment.

He considered the consternation it would cause to know that a serving Officer had sunk to the level of a common thief.

Every aspect of the story passed through his mind.

He saw that it would not be a short-lived incident.

It could have far-reaching consequences which

would be disastrous in more ways than one.

There was silence for so long that at last Gina said in a nervous voice:

"I . . . I am sorry to . . . bother you with this . . . you must have so many . . . other things . . . to worry about . . . but I could not think of anyone else to whom I could . . . turn or whom I could . . . ask for help."

"You were quite right to come to me," the Marquis said, "and it was very intelligent of you to realise that it would be disastrous not only for your Mother and Captain Dawes, but also for your Father's Regiment, if it became common knowledge."

"That is . . . what I thought," Gina said, "and I know that Papa, who was very . . . proud of the Life Guards, would . . . dislike having anything . . . disparaging said about it or . . . the Officers who serve in it."

"I find it hard to believe that Dawes would really sink so low as to steal," the Marquis said.

"As he has . . . already taken so much . . . money from Mama," Gina said, "it seems . . . strange that he should also need to . . . steal things from the house such as the . . . gold seal which he put into his pocket. I thought . . . before he left the house he might return it to the desk, but it was not there."

"You are sure of that?" the Marquis asked.

"I went into the Morning-Room while I was waiting for the carriage to come round to bring me here," Gina said. "The seal was . . . not on the desk or . . . anywhere else."

"As you so rightly say, Miss Lang, this sort of thing cannot go on," the Marquis remarked.

"You will speak to Captain Dawes?" Gina asked. "He will of course deny it!"

"That is what I was thinking myself," the Marquis agreed, "and we have no proof, unless of course what he has stolen is still in his possession, or he has sold it to some well-known shop."

"I realize that," Gina said, "and I have locked the cases and taken away the keys. But the boxes which are missing are four of the most . . . valuable and which Papa was . . . proudest of . . . owning."

"I know exactly what you are feeling," the Marquis said, "and it is what I too should feel if any of my collections had been interfered with."

Gina glanced round the room thinking there were a great many beautiful possessions in it.

Then she told herself she was not concerned with the Marquis, but with her Mother's friendship with a despicable young man.

Captain Dawes ought to be drummed out of his Regiment.

Yet she knew the Marquis was right in saying that a scandal about an Officer in any Regiment of the Household Cavalry was to be avoided.

Especially so at this moment when a large number of his Regiment were abroad fighting against Napoleon.

"What are . . . we to . . . do?" she asked in a whisper.

69

"It is a problem which I intend to solve," the Marquis replied, "but the difficulty, as you know yourself, is how we can do it and when."

"And you will really . . . help me?"

The Marquis smiled.

"You know the answer to that. I am going to help you, but I want you to trust me, Miss Lang, if I do it in a different way from what you expect. It will certainly be as secretly and quietly as possible so that no one knows about it except you and me."

"Oh . . . thank you . . . thank . . . you!" Gina cried. "I lay . . . awake last night . . . wondering desperately what I . . . could do . . . and now you have . . . answered my . . . prayers."

"I thought you might have been praying about it," the Marquis said.

He thought as he spoke that it was an unusual thing for him to say.

He wondered how he knew that this young girl prayed, not just with her lips, but also with her heart.

Yet he did know, and he thought the way she spoke was somehow very moving.

The expression in her eyes had changed.

It seemed as if she looked upon him as some sort of Archangel come down from Heaven to assist her.

The Marquis had been looked at passionately, admiringly, and sometimes with fury by many women.

But, he thought, it was the first time that anyone had looked at him as if he was a god from Olympus.

Or perhaps a Knight in Shining Armour re-solved to kill the dragon which no other man would tackle.

As he did not speak Gina said after a moment:

"Wh-what do . . . you suggest . . . we do?"

"That is what I am trying to decide," the Mar-quis replied.

He gave a sudden exclamation.

"I have it!" he said. "The first step is for me to meet Dawes and find out if he is as bad as you think he is without his being aware that he is under surveillance."

"How can . . . you do . . . that?" Gina asked.

"I am giving a party at Arrowhead, which is my house in the country, at the end of the week," the Marquis said. "I will send an invitation to your Mother asking her to be one of my guests and to bring you with her. I could explain that having known your Father I am anxious to meet his daughter."

Gina was listening wide-eyed and the Marquis went on:

"I will send an invitation also to Captain Dawes who, I feel, will not refuse it."

There was a sarcastic note in the Marquis's voice as he spoke.

He knew that invitations to Arrowhead were prized by everybody.

Even the Prince Regent had never been known to refuse to be his guest.

"If you do that then you will see . . . Captain Dawes for . . . yourself," Gina was saying, "and of course Mama will be . . . delighted that he is invited."

The Marquis put to her the next question as tactfully as he could.

"Surely your Mother," he said, "finds someone as young as Dawes an inadequate companion after the brilliance of your Father's intellect?"

"That is what I thought myself when I first saw him," Gina admitted. "But when I was thinking it over last night I understood. Papa, you see, was very much older than Mama and, although she loved him dearly, I think sometimes she had difficulty in . . . understanding his . . . brilliance and his . . . wit."

She looked away from the Marquis shyly before she went on:

"Captain Dawes delights Mama with his extravagant, over-dramatic compliments, and seldom . . . talks of . . . anything except . . . her."

The Marquis thought it was extremely intelligent of Gina to have worked this out for herself.

It was what he had suspected, and she had put it into words.

He also thought that if, as he imagined, Dawes was tricking Lady Langdale into giving him so much money, he had found a clever way of doing so.

"At Arrowhead I can keep my eye on Dawes," he said aloud, "and see what he gets up to. I will invite some men who are older and more trustworthy and will undoubtedly admire your Mother and make her happy."

"How can . . . you be so . . . wonderful?" Gina asked and her voice broke on the last word. "I felt so . . . desperate and so . . . inadequate to cope with this . . . alone, and now you are doing exactly what I . . . wanted you to . . . do."

"Just trust me," the Marquis said, "and again let me assure you that what we have talked about will not be repeated outside this room."

Gina got to her feet.

"I have taken up too much of your time when you are so busy," she said, "and I only wish I could . . . express my gratitude in adequate words."

The Marquis thought of saying he could read what she felt in her eyes now that she was no longer afraid.

Then he thought that perhaps she would think he was paying her a compliment.

Because of the behaviour of Dawes towards her Mother, it was obviously something at the moment that would shock her.

He walked with her to the door.

Just before he opened it he said:

"Do nothing and say nothing until we meet at Arrowhead on Friday. We want to catch Dawes redhanded, so it would be a mistake for him to suspect what is in our minds."

"I will be very . . . very careful not to . . . arouse his . . . suspicion that I am . . . watching him," Gina murmured.

"A lot depends upon our catching him unawares, and that is what we have to do," the Marquis said. "If we can, perhaps I will be able to settle everything quietly without anyone, especially your Mother, being aware of it."

"That is what I . . . pray will . . . happen," Gina said, "but Mama is so trusting. She believes the best of everyone and is always surprised and shocked if anyone does her anything . . . wrong."

"Then we must both try to protect her from men like Dawes, or anybody else who might make her unhappy," the Marquis said.

He saw the adoration in Gina's eyes and knew he had put into words what she was thinking.

He thought it was extraordinary how he could read her thoughts.

He opened the door and they crossed the Hall to where there were two footmen on duty.

The Marquis took Gina out onto the doorstep.

She put her hand in his.

As she felt its vibrations she knew that he was good and noble.

It was just as she had known, when she had first shaken hands with Captain Dawes, that there was something wrong with him.

"Good-bye, Miss Lang," the Marquis said. "It has been a great pleasure to meet you."

"Good-bye, and thank you . . . thank you!" Gina replied.

She dropped him a small and graceful curtsy before she stepped into her carriage.

The footman shut the door and she drove away.

The Marquis turned and walked back into the house and along the passage to the Study.

Harry was sitting comfortably in one of the leather armchairs reading the newspaper.

"You have been a long time," he complained as the Marquis came into the room. "How much did it cost you?"

"Nothing, as it happens," the Marquis replied, "but I did not realise that Miss Lang's Father was Lord Langdale of Lavon. You must remember him?"

"Of course I remember him," Harry said. "He came to the Barracks quite often when I first joined the Regiment. I always thought him an extremely clever and interesting man."

"His daughter is intelligent too," the Marquis said, "and as I feel I ought to do something about Lady Langdale, who is now out of mourning, I have asked them to Arrowhead on Friday."

"If you are asking Lady Langdale, you had better ask her constant companion," Harry replied. "I do not suppose you have ever met Guy Dawes, who is a slick young Beau who fancies himself at the card-table."

"How do you know all this?" the Marquis enquired.

"I have seen him the last two or three times I have been in White's, and several people have told me that he gambles for high stakes although they think he has not actually much in his pocket."

The Marquis thought this was exactly the sort

of information he wanted to hear.

He had however no intention of breaking his promise to Gina and telling Harry the purpose of her visit.

"I want you to come to Arrowhead and I expect you to help me entertain the house-party," the Marquis said. "Incidentally, I have some new horses I would like you to see."

"That is an invitation I would not think of refusing," Harry replied. "Who else are you going to invite?"

"I was wondering about that," the Marquis replied. "I suppose Imogen, for one."

"I knew that would be inevitable," Harry joked, "and who are you asking for me?"

"Who would you like?" the Marquis enquired.

"Someone beautiful, sophisticated, and willing to cheer up a poor soldier who has not seen a pretty woman for months!"

The Marquis laughed.

"You shall have your wish, and I can think of at least half-a-dozen women who would fit your requirements with ease."

"Then ask them all!" Harry said. "What are we keeping ourselves for? There is always the chance, as you well know, that Napoleon will invade us and we will merely become a French Colony."

"I have never heard of anything so defeatist!" the Marquis said. "If you are not careful, you will find yourself being taken to the Tower and shot for inciting England to surrender!"

Harry laughed.

"If you want the truth, I think the war has already come to an end and there is no need for us to worry any further. Napoleon was really beaten at Trafalgar."

"Unfortunately he does not think so," the Marquis replied. "While you are treating it lightly, Harry, there is still a chance, although I admit it is a small one, that, as cornered rats will fight desperately, we might find that the man who has conquered almost the whole of Europe will win in the end."

The Marquis spoke seriously.

He was thinking as he spoke that until Napoleon was behind bars there would never be the peace that everybody was praying for.

He remembered at the same time how Gina had said he was the answer to her prayers.

He was sure she also prayed that Wellington would finally defeat Bonaparte.

He did not say anything aloud.

But his thoughts went to the terrible slaughter that had been caused already by Napoleon's Armies.

It was not only the loss of men that he minded so desperately when he was on the battlefield.

It was the screams of the horses that echoed in his mind night after night.

It also hurt him unbearably to see men wounded and blood-stained.

They would be piled into an empty Church or a dirty, unsanitary house without doctors to tend to their wounds.

War, he had often told himself, was not just winning a victory over an enemy.

It was the terrible suffering and slaughter of human beings.

Seeing the fear in Gina's eyes had reminded him of the peasant women that he and his men had seen as they entered a village in Portugal.

The Portuguese were never certain whether the English came as friends or foes.

When he left Portugal, they were moving through drenched fields, marching under blazing suns, weighed down with knapsacks, flint-lock muskets and ball-cartridges.

In the mountain villages the houses were so full of vermin that if a man lay down he was certain to be bitten from head to foot.

Yet these hard-used men were filled with a burning love of their Country.

They went into battle with shouts of "Hurrah for Old England" and with drums beating the advance.

At Albuera two-thirds of the Gloucesters and all their Officers had fallen.

Yet he remembered how one of the Sergeants, finding he could still stagger, hobbled back into the fight.

"Now which men shall we invite," he asked, "besides, as you suggested, young Dawes?"

"You are not really asking him to Arrowhead, are you?" Harry exclaimed. "He is not 'up to scratch,' I can assure you of that!"

"If Lady Langdale wants him, we had better

have him," the Marquis replied, "and if we need intelligent conversation, I will ask my Uncle William, and I will send an invitation to Castlereagh."

"The Foreign Secretary?" Harry exclaimed. "I feel he ought not to be taking time off from the Ministry. But doubtless an invitation to Arrowhead would tempt him, as it would tempt anyone with any sense."

"Thank you, Harry!" the Marquis replied wryly.

"Now do not be modest, Hengis," Harry said. "You know you have the finest house in the whole country. What more could anyone want?"

"The answer to that — for you at any rate — is pretty women!" the Marquis replied. "And I am making a list of them."

chapter four

Lady Imogen Strangway looked at herself in the mirror with satisfaction.

Her hair, arranged in a new fashion, had blue lights in it.

Her eyes, with their touch of green, were very large and her skin was dazzlingly white.

She thought it would be difficult for any man to resist her, and in particular the Marquis of Mortlake.

At twenty-eight Lady Imogen knew she was at the height of her beauty.

She was aware, and she was really very critical, that she had never looked as entrancing as she had these last months.

At the same time she was sensible enough to know that beauty does not last.

She could see it fading in many of her contemporaries.

Certainly those a year or two older were already beginning to look as if they were past their best.

She knew that what she had to do was to be married.

She intended with an iron determination to

marry the Marquis of Mortlake.

There was nobody in the world of the *Beau Monde* who was more suitable, she thought, to be her husband.

There was nobody, for that matter, she wanted more as a man.

Lady Imogen had had a very chequered past.

It was only by a miracle that she had not been annihilated socially when she was a debutante.

Her father, Gordon Chester, was a Cousin of the Duke of Milchester.

He was not well off, for his parents, having given him a good education, could provide him with only a small allowance.

He therefore decided, because he enjoyed travelling and was also proficient in foreign languages, to join the Diplomatic Corps.

His antecedents and his relationship to the Duke assured his being accepted.

Before the French Revolution he spent some years in France.

After that, until Napoleon Bonaparte appeared on the horizon, he was posted in several different countries, enjoying the experience.

Gordon Chester made no outstanding contribution, neither did he win much promotion in the Service.

Then came the war and he was recalled to London.

He had been married in 1784 to a very beautiful woman who accompanied him on his postings abroad.

She had her looks and a little money of her own, but they had little in common.

He was therefore not particularly stricken when she died of a foreign fever for which no doctor could find a cure.

Gordon Chester was left with his only child, a daughter called Imogen.

He sent her to School in London while he was working in the Foreign Office.

In 1802 the Treaty of Amiens was signed with Napoleon, which brought peace after nine years of strife.

Gordon Chester was bored with England and serving under a number of Diplomats older and wiser than himself, so he begged and pleaded to be sent to France.

Because the Duke of Milchester intervened on his behalf, he achieved his desire.

He set off excitedly, taking Imogen, who was now seventeen, with him.

For her it was the most exciting thing that had ever happened.

She had become weary of the Seminary for Young Ladies in which she had been educated.

She had found it constricting.

It was also tantalising because most of the girls were far richer than she was and had many more gowns.

They also had parents who entertained for them during the holidays.

She did not miss her mother particularly.

Already, rather like her father, she had become

self-centered and egotistical.

She was concerned only with herself and whatever was happening at the moment.

The idea of going to Paris thrilled her.

She begged or borrowed what clothes she could
from her richer friends.

At last she could be able to cope with what
she was told to her surprise was a very *chic* Society.

When they set out from England, both Gordon
Chester and his daughter found everything a surprise.

The ragged rabble of Calais who waited on the
Quayside stretched out welcoming, if dirty,
hands.

They politely helped the English milords down
the landing-ladders of the ship which had
brought them across the Channel.

Gordon Chester had been warned by his
friends before he and Imogen left that they would
have to endure an unmitigated diet of frogs.

He discovered however that the new France
was not worse, but better, than the France he
had known in the past.

Instead of the villainous *sansculottes* and blood-
stained scenes of Gilray's cartoons, they found
friendly faces everywhere.

The streets were clean and the Citizens appeared to be well-behaved.

Imogen thought the women in their red camlet
jackets and high aprons, with long flying lappets
to their caps, looked very attractive.

The journey south to Paris confirmed their first impressions.

There was no waste land, the peasant women and children looked well-fed.

The grooms at the Post-houses and the people along the road were good-natured.

There were, of course, monuments to the Revolution.

At Abbeville the larger houses were shut up and the streets were full of beggars.

The magnificent Castle of Chantilly was in ruins and its beautiful garden laid waste.

It was in Paris that the "Grand Nation" could be seen in all its charm and glory.

The new approach through the squalid suburbs was imposing.

The Norman Barrier with massive Doric pillars, the long avenues of elms.

And beyond the Place de la Concorde — which had been the Place de la Revolution — the Tuileries.

Paris, Imogen and her father found, had become a City of beauty and pleasure.

The horror and reeking murder of the Terror had been forgotten.

Gardens, dance-halls and restaurants graced the palaces of the former Nobility.

The Bois with its horses and carriages, the great new shops with their silks and trimmings, furniture, bronzes and china, were enticing.

Gordon Chester found it all hard to believe, and to his daughter it was a revelation.

Almost from the moment they arrived, they were swept into a whirlpool of gaiety which left Imogen breathless.

Napoleon Bonaparte, who never missed anything that was going on, learnt of the arrival of the Duke of Milchester's Cousin.

He invited Gordon Chester and his daughter to the Tuileries Palace.

Gordon, who remembered Versailles in the old days, thought he had never seen such magnificence as the First Consul's apartment.

There appeared to be hundreds of footmen in their green and gold liveries.

The gorgeously be-gilt peace Officers paraded about, vying with the uniforms of the *Aides-de-Camp* in Courtly splendour.

To Imogen the dominating figure, as to every other English visitor, was that of the First Consul.

It was only a few months since England had seen him drawn by the Cartoonists as an unshaven, common Corsican, born in a hovel.

The cartoons showed him looting, burning and murdering.

Now they saw him as the greatest man in Europe, taking the salute of his troops with all the pomp and splendour of Royalty.

Imogen watched him riding a horse that had belonged to the late King of France.

He passed down the lines with cropped hair, a high nose and searching eyes.

Imogen was having a wonderful time.

She was thrilled by the frivolous and inexhaustible gaiety of the Society to which she and her father were introduced.

There were a large number of fascinating Frenchmen to pay her the first compliments she had ever received.

They whispered words of love she had never heard before.

It would have been impossible for any young girl to resist the excitement of it all.

It was then that Imogen met one of Napoleon's up-and-coming Commanders — Pierre Ribeau.

He was dark-haired, good-looking in the French fashion, and had the "honeyed tongue" of his race.

Any woman would have found him irresistible.

Imogen fell in love with him, and he seduced her.

She was in fact only too willing to be seduced.

Then, before she and her father had been many months in Paris, she was forced to tell him that she was having a baby.

Gordon Chester was horrified.

Because he had been intent on enjoying himself he had not realised how his daughter was behaving.

In the very comfortable apartment they rented near the British Embassy he used to see her at breakfast.

Then they met again, usually before dinner, when they were both dressing to go out with their own friends.

It had never struck him that for most of the

time Imogen was not properly chaperoned.

Not that she relied on the men who admired her to take her from party to party.

That she had been exclusively with Pierre Ribeau for the last three months had escaped his notice.

There was no question of Imogen marrying Ribeau for the simple reason that he was already married.

He was a Catholic, and he had several children.

"What shall I do, Papa?" Imogen asked.

She looked so beautiful as she asked the question that her father found it difficult to be angry with her.

He was however not a Diplomat for nothing.

He looked quickly and carefully at the other men who found her attractive.

Captain Richard Strangway was the Officer-in-Charge of the Military Guard at the British Embassy.

He came of a good family.

His father was a Baronet and he had a certain amount of money.

Gordon Chester took Richard Strangway into his confidence.

"I am worried about my daughter," he said, "because I am so busy, diplomatically speaking, that I have not the time to look after her as I should."

He made a helpless gesture as he went on:

"It is difficult for me being a widower, and there is no one in England with whom Imogen would be as happy as she is with me."

He sighed before he went on:

"At the same time, I think she is moving in rather a fast set, which is not really suitable for a young girl."

Richard Strangway agreed with every word.

He thought Imogen was very lovely and it was not right for her to be unchaperoned.

He admired Imogen and it was only a week or so before he was completely and hopelessly in love.

Gordon Chester was delighted.

He suggested to Richard Strangway that as he might be moved from his present post, he should marry Imogen before anybody else "snapped her up."

He was only too willing to do so, and they were married at the British Embassy Church.

They received an expensive wedding-present from the First Consul.

They were also invited to dinner at the Tuileries Palace as soon as they returned from their honeymoon.

The First Consul drank to their health.

He made a speech hoping they would be blessed as he had been when he had married Josephine.

The announcement of the marriage appeared in *The Gazette* in England.

Imogen received letters of congratulation from many of the Chester family.

The Duke wrote bluntly:

I am delighted to hear that you are marrying an Englishman and have not lost your head and your heart to some 'Frenchie'! We also hear that the peace will not last, but I optimistically believe that the Corsican has had enough of war to satisfy him, and we shall have no more trouble.

It was a wish that was not to be granted.

Early in the next year Richard Strangway was obliged to bring his wife back to England.

She found the long journey exhausting.

She had only recently given birth to what was published as a premature baby.

The child was still-born and Imogen was very ill for several weeks.

When they arrived back in England they stayed with Richard Strangway's family who had never met his bride.

Hostilities between the French and the English started up with a ferocity that seemed even worse than ever before.

Imogen had gone home, but her father was still in France.

He was therefore aware how tense was the relationship between England and the First Consul.

Addington, the Prime Minister, had started to re-arm under pressure from some members of Parliament.

They were afraid that war might break out again, and the country would not be prepared for it.

On Sunday, March 13, in a Parisian Drawing-Room, Bonaparte bore down on Lord Charles Whilworth, the British Ambassador, in the presence of a large gathering, shouting:

"So, you are bent on war!"

The astonished Ambassador replied that England after fighting for nine years was very anxious for peace.

Bonaparte retorted with:

"Now you mean to force me to fight for fifteen more years!"

He told the Russian and the Spanish Ambassadors that the British did not keep their word.

Then he walked back again to Lord Charles waving his stick so that the tall, stately Englishman thought he was about to strike him.

"If you arm," Bonaparte shouted, "I will arm too. If you fight, I will fight also. You think to destroy France. You will never intimidate her!"

The Ambassador tried to pour oil on troubled waters without avail.

On May 18, Napoleon, in a towering rage, ordered the arrest of all British travellers in France.

Thousands of British citizens were seized, some, like Sir Richard Addington's son, as he disembarked at Calais and landed on French soil.

One infatuated Baronet was incarcerated for eleven years because he delayed for a few hours to enjoy the favours of a very attractive Parisienne.

The future Duke of Argyll managed to escape

across the Swiss/German frontier disguised as a chambermaid.

Internment of civilians was contrary to all civilised precedent.

It made the English more convinced than ever that they were dealing with an untutored savage.

Gordon Chester was fortunate enough to be allowed, as a Diplomat, to leave the country.

He found his daughter hysterical after news of Napoleon's repudiation of the treaty had reached London fearing something had happened to him.

He also found that she was on her own.

Her husband had been recalled to his Regiment and was in Barracks.

Imogen therefore was quite willing to play hostess for her father.

Two years later this became very much to her liking.

The Duke of Milchester died without a direct heir.

His only son had been killed in a riding accident two months previously.

To his astonishment Gordon Chester became the 3rd Duke of Milchester.

It gave Imogen the place in Society she had always wanted.

She entertained not only in Milchester House in London, but also in Chester Castle in Hampshire.

Unfortunately she and her father discovered that there was very little money to inherit.

Certainly not enough to keep up the pomp and

comfort expected in the Ducal houses.

The following year Richard Strangway was drowned at sea in a ship carrying British troops to the Mediterranean.

Imogen was not particularly distressed.

She had already begun to find her husband a bore.

She had turned to the fascinating men she met in London who congregated round the Prince of Wales and in the Clubs of St. James's.

Most of them were of course serving their country in various capacities.

Of these, some could not join the Army or the Navy for one reason or another.

Imogen chose the richest and most attractive of them to be her lovers.

As the years passed she became very experienced at handling them.

Her expertise at enticing a man was irresistible.

She was by now planning her life carefully for the future.

She knew that it was imperative she should marry again, both for the right Social position and also to someone who was very rich.

This paragon was not as easy to find as she expected.

The members of English Aristocracy, like the French, married off their eldest sons early to the "right type of girl."

It ensured the succession of the title.

The mothers of suitable young women were only too delighted to get them off their hands.

There were many men who admired Imogen and with whom she had passionate and satisfying *affaires de coeur*.

They were however not in a position to offer her a wedding-ring.

She encouraged them to offer her a number of other things.

The war was causing the Milchester estates to deteriorate even faster than before.

"What the devil are we going to do?" the new Duke asked his daughter over and over again.

"I gave you quite a lot of money a month ago," Imogen answered. "I can hardly ask again for so much so quickly."

"The point is," her father would reply, "that I cannot pay the wages and we are short of servants as it is."

They were also short of labourers on the farms, horses in the stables, and carriages with which to convey them from London to the country.

"If I walk about in rags," Imogen remarked on one occasion, "no one will look at me twice, and we shall be even harder up than we are at the moment."

She became known as the most expensive woman in London.

That did not however deter the number of men who were perfectly prepared to pay for their pleasure, as long as it was a pleasure.

No one who made love to Imogen could say that they were not satisfied.

But there were undoubtedly a number of men

who retired to the country, finding that enough could often be too much, when it came to Imogen.

She had not yet met the Marquis of Mortlake, but she had of course heard about him.

When he was wounded and came back from Portugal, the newspapers were full of the stories of his gallantry and of his great possessions.

Even before she saw him Imogen was interested.

As soon as she did see him, she knew that here was her fate and exactly what she required.

For some time after he came home the Marquis was allowed no visitors apart from his family.

As he got better he was determined to go to the War Office to ask them to send him back to the Peninsula.

He began to appear at several small parties which would not be too tiring.

He had no idea that his every movement was known to Lady Imogen by some method or another.

But he did find her at almost every party he attended, whether it was luncheon or dinner.

He was used to women looking at him with inviting eyes.

Therefore he did not take any particular notice of Imogen to begin with.

This made her more determined than ever that she would become a part of his life.

Gradually the Marquis began to appreciate not only her beauty, which he could not help admiring, but also her wit.

He enjoyed the sharp-pointed manner in which her brain worked.

He was, of course, well aware that she was pursuing him.

At the moment however he had no other interests in the way of a beautiful woman.

He was therefore prepared to accept what the gods, or rather Imogen, had to offer him.

He found her the most passionate and the most insatiable woman he had ever known.

At the same time, because she was so experienced, she took care not to demand too much too quickly.

Above all, to make sure he was not bored.

"He is mine! He is mine!" she would tell herself triumphantly after he had become her lover.

When morning came, however, and he left her, she always had the anxious feeling that he was still elusive.

What was more, she still had not heard the four words she wanted so desperately to hear.

When he would ask her to become his wife.

"He has to marry me, he has to!" she told her reflection in the mirror.

But she knew when he left her bedroom that nothing was certain.

The Marquis excited her more than any man she had ever known.

She knew he felt the same about her.

But he had never once said that he loved her, and she knew that while she possessed his body, she did not possess his heart.

To-night he was dining alone with her at Milchester House.

She had gone to a great deal of trouble and expense to provide him with a meal that consisted of all his favourite dishes.

The champagne was the best procurable.

It was somewhat difficult to obtain since the war had broken out again.

The brandy, which was excellent, had been smuggled in from France.

Imogen, as it happened, knew a great deal about smuggling.

This was one way by which she had been able to supply her father with the money he needed so urgently.

She was not perturbed by the fact that the smugglers who operated from almost every cove in the South of England were taking gold coinage to France.

This helped Napoleon to pursue the war which had grown more violent and more expensive than it had ever been before.

Rising from the dressing-table Imogen let her maid help her into the gown she had chosen to wear.

It was very attractive with a high waist revealing the perfection of her rounded breasts.

The transparency of the full skirt did little to disguise her narrow hips.

It was an extremely expensive gown.

It was trimmed with roses sparkling with

diamante and satin ribbons which had certainly been smuggled in from France.

"Ye looks lovely, M'Lady!" the maid said as she finished fastening the gown at the back.

It was a compliment that the woman made every evening to keep her mistress in a good temper.

"Do you really think so, Bessie?" Lady Imogen asked.

"Oi've never seen Yer Ladyship look lovelier!" Bessie said.

There was a smile of satisfaction on Imogen's perfectly shaped lips as she left the bedroom.

Only when she had gone did Bessie murmur to herself:

"Her'll be lucky if she gets 'im, an' unlucky fer 'im, poor devil!"

Lady Imogen reached the top of the stairs.

She saw that the man-servant was opening the front door and knew that the Marquis had arrived.

She did not move, but stood poised in the candlelight.

She made an exquisite picture at the top of the staircase which curved down into the Hall.

As the Marquis handed his top-hat and cape to the Butler he looked up at her.

For a moment they were both still and did not speak.

Then slowly Imogen came down the stairs.

She advanced with a snake-like movement that was graceful and at the same time alluring.

When she reached the Marquis she held out her hand, and he kissed her fingers.

"You are here!" she breathed in a soft, seductive voice. "I have been waiting all day and I thought the hours would never pass."

"Now, they have," the Marquis replied in a matter-of-fact tone, "and I must tell you that you look very beautiful."

"That is what I hoped you would think," Imogen replied.

They walked to the small Sitting-Room on the Ground Floor.

It was small and therefore easier to make attractive than the larger Drawing-Room on the First Floor which was badly in need of repair.

Imogen had ordered flowers and they scented the room.

The candles, discreetly placed, did not reveal how threadbare the carpet was and how faded the curtains.

Anyway it would be impossible for any man, she thought, not to look at her alone.

As the door shut behind them, Imogen moved closer to the Marquis.

"It seems a century, Dearest, wonderful Hengis, since you kissed me."

The Marquis bent his head.

As he did so he wondered why he remembered little Gina Lang calling him "wonderful."

The dinner was good, but not as delicious as if it had been cooked by one of his own superlative Chefs.

The Marquis realised that Imogen was doing her best to entertain him.

He knew it would be churlish of him not to be delighted, as she hoped.

She related little tidbits of gossip about their friends which made him laugh.

She speculated on several romances in a witty, if rather unkind manner, but which he could not help finding extremely amusing.

When they left the Dining-Room together she said:

"Shall we go upstairs? I have something to show you, and also why should we waste time when I want you? Oh, Hengis, how much I want you!"

There seemed no point in not agreeing.

Yet the Marquis disliked the idea that she was taking the initiative.

It was for him to pursue her rather than be pursued.

He had the sudden and uncomfortable feeling that, like so many of his other ardent love-affairs, this one was beginning to pall on him.

Then he told himself he was being nonsensical.

No one could be more satisfying or exciting than Imogen.

He would be very ungrateful not to admit that he had enjoyed the time they had spent together since his shoulder had healed.

When he entered her bedroom he found the candles burning in exactly the right positions.

There was in the air the scent of her exotic

French perfume which reminded him of Paris.

Imogen with her hair fully over her white shoulders was leaning her head against the lace caped pillows.

He wanted to protest that what they were doing was what she desired rather than what he wanted.

"Am I a man, or a mouse?" he asked silently in the same way he might have asked it of Harry.

He was also annoyed with himself for being ungrateful.

It annoyed him to know that he was disappointing somebody who had done everything in her power to please him.

He forced himself therefore to concentrate on Imogen's beauty.

To feel the fire that shone in her eyes was complemented by the fire rising within himself.

For the first time since he had known Imogen it was an effort.

When the Marquis was walking home just before dawn he thought with a sense of relief that in two days' time he would be going to Arrowhead.

He had asked Imogen at dinner to come as one of his guests and she had said:

"But, of course, Darling. It is something I would love to do, and you know I enjoy playing hostess to your friends."

She had given him a sideways glance and there was a smile on her lips as she said:

"You always tell me that I do it beautifully and

exactly what is expected of the Chatelaine of Arrowhead."

The Marquis understood exactly what she meant.

It was an invitation for him to reply that that would be her position for the rest of her life.

Instead he answered:

"I cannot promise that you will do that on this occasion. I am giving the party for Lady Langdale, who has just come out of mourning. She is older than you, and I may also invite one of my relatives."

Imogen gave a cry of horror.

"That would spoil everything!" she said. "You know your relatives are old and boring and do not really approve of you — or me!"

The Marquis thought that was untrue where he was concerned.

They certainly disapproved of Imogen, as did most older women in the Social round.

"As for Lady Langdale," Imogen said scornfully, "she may have been beautiful once, and of course when her husband was alive they were of some importance. But now she is making a fool of herself with a ghastly young man called Guy Dawes. I suppose she pays him for sitting at her feet like a tame poodle!"

The Marquis thought that Imogen had inadvertently stumbled on the truth.

She had no idea that this was the reason why he was giving the party.

"I think you are being hard on Lady Langdale," he said, "and I am also going to ask her daughter who has just left School."

"You really are crucifying yourself!" Imogen exclaimed. "You know you hate young girls. You had better ask some chinless young men to keep her company, otherwise she may get in our way."

The Marquis did not reply.

He changed the subject and merely talked to Imogen about herself.

For a moment she forgot the party and the part she wished to play in it.

As the Marquis turned into Park Lane he saw the rising sun shine on the trees in Hyde Park.

It made him think how beautiful Arrowhead would look.

He then thought that, as his party had been arranged in order to help Gina, it had been a mistake to include Imogen.

She would, however, be likely to turn up anyway.

He realised she had been manoeuvring herself into a position where she behaved as if she owned him.

She could take liberties which no one else would dare to do.

"I am getting myself into a mess," he thought.

He was frowning as he reached the entrance to the drive to his front door.

chapter five

Gina appreciated the way the journey to Arrowhead was arranged down to every detail.

Although they started with their own horses,
every ten miles they changed them at a Posting
Inn for the Marquis's well-bred horses to be put
between the shafts.

He owned a house which was just half-way
from London to Arrowhead which was on the
coast.

It was not a very large house, but it was very
comfortable and they found that several other of
the Marquis's guests were staying the night there.

There were maid-servants to look after them
and the food they had for dinner was delicious.

They all left early the next morning in their
various carriages.

Gina and her Mother arrived at Arrowhead at
exactly the expected time of four o'clock.

A large and elaborate tea was waiting for them
and Lady Imogen was there to act as hostess.

She greeted Lady Langdale very pleasantly, but
gave Gina, when she saw how pretty she was, a
rather hard glance.

They and the other guests, as they arrived, clustered round the tea-table.

Lady Imogen made it very clear that she was very much at home at Arrowhead.

"This is such a lovely house," she said. "I was thinking this is my tenth visit and I really feel it is just like home to me."

The way she spoke made one or two of the other guests look at each other knowingly.

Gina knew instinctively that she intended to become the Marquis's wife.

Arrowhead itself was even more beautiful than she had expected.

When they had stayed the night on the way, one of the guests, a middle-aged man, had told her the history of it.

"It has always been believed," he said, "that when William the Conqueror was approaching England with his troops in a number of ships, one of his commanders called duLac said boastfully:

" 'It is obviously a very pretty island. I will build a Castle on it.'

"One of the other men had replied:

" 'You will have to conquer it first!'

" 'That will not be difficult,' he said, 'and to show you that I mean what I say, I will choose the place now where I will build my home.'

"He called an Archer and taking his bow from him he drew back the arrow.

"He was, as it happens, one of the outstanding Archers in Normandy.

"The arrow flew through the air and when it fell to the ground he said:

" 'That is where I will lay my foundations.'

"The Castle that was built there was called Arrowhead. Although the original castle was pulled down, over the centuries other Castles and houses have been built on the same site and the name has remained unchanged."

Gina thought it was a very romantic story, and she could understand that the Marquis was exceedingly proud of his home.

He did not appear at tea-time, but Lady Imogen told the guests that he was riding.

"Do men ever do anything else?" she asked. "Except of course shoot and fish!"

She spoke provocatively, looking at the Gentlemen in the party as she spoke.

One of the Ladies said quietly:

"They also fight, and Hengis has certainly played his part on the battlefield."

It was a rebuke and Gina saw Lady Imogen flush angrily.

For a moment her green eyes seemed to gleam with fire.

It was then that Gina was aware that Lady Imogen was dangerous.

It was her instinct telling her so, and she realised it was not obvious to everyone else.

In fact Lady Imogen went out of her way to make herself charming to all the guests as they arrived one after another.

Gina saw that all the Ladies were extremely

pretty and the Gentlemen distinguished.

Then Viscount Castlereagh arrived.

He sat down next to Gina with a cup of tea in his hand, and said:

"I cannot tell you, Miss Lang, how much I miss your Father. He was always very kind to me when I was a young man. I turned to him with many problems and difficulties and he always helped me."

"I like hearing you say that," Gina replied, "and I too miss Papa more than I can ever tell you."

"I can understand that," Lord Castlereagh said.

They started to talk of the help her Father had been to many famous men.

When the Marquis came in he was surprised to see the Foreign Secretary talking animatedly to his youngest and least important guest.

He had always seemed somewhat shy.

As he greeted Gina she thought how kind he was to include her and her Mother in this exciting party.

From the way the Marquis looked at her and the pressure of his fingers on hers, she felt he was reassuring her.

It was as if he was telling her that the troubles that had brought them together could somehow be solved at Arrowhead.

'I hope he is right,' she thought.

Then, as he left her to talk to some other guests, she went on conversing with the Viscount.

When the Ladies went up to dress, Gina would have been gratified if she had known that Viscount Castlereagh said to the Marquis:

"I am delighted to have been able to meet Lord Langdale's daughter. She is the most intelligent woman I have had the pleasure of talking to for a long time."

The Marquis looked at him in surprise.

"I do not think Miss Lang is a year over eighteen."

"Age does not matter," the Viscount replied, "it is brains that count. She undoubtedly has her Father's intelligence, and a way of expressing herself that makes me feel we must somehow get her on the Political platform."

The Marquis was even more surprised.

At the same time he told himself this was something he should have discovered about Gina.

It would certainly be a help in the problem she had set him regarding Guy Dawes.

Because of his Regimental duties, Guy Dawes had arrived very late at the house where they had stayed overnight.

Apparently he had over-slept the next morning.

Lady Langdale complained because he was not down for breakfast.

They even had to leave without him.

"He has his own phaeton, Mama," Gina reasoned, "and I expect he will catch up with us quite easily."

"I hope so," Lady Langdale replied. "The dear

boy is so looking forward to staying at Arrowhead that it would be disastrous if anything prevented him from getting there."

Gina knew her Mother was really hoping that he would travel with them.

She persuaded her that it would be a mistake to alter at the last moment what arrangements Captain Dawes had made.

Finally they drove away without seeing him.

Now as he kissed Lady Langdale's hand and burst into an effusive apology for being so late, Gina watched her Mother relax.

She was thankful that the tension which had made her indifferent to everybody else had passed.

As they went in to dinner she realised that the Marquis had cleverly placed her Mother on his right.

Another young Lady, even though she had a higher rank, was seated on his left.

Because it saved trouble, he had allowed Imogen to sit at the other end of the table and act as hostess.

She made the very most of her position, making it clear to everyone that she was in control and the Marquis could not manage without her.

After dinner they moved from the stately and very impressive Dining-Room into the Drawing-Room.

It was an exquisitely furnished room.

The pictures were breathtaking and there were what Gina thought of as treasures everywhere she looked.

She was aware that the Ladies were gossiping about their friends in London whom she did not know.

They talked of the parties at which they had met them the previous week.

Because she knew she had nothing to add to the conversation she moved about looking at some exquisite pieces of Dresden china and of jade which were very old and she was certain had a history.

There was also a collection of snuff-boxes that rivalled her father's.

She saw that the Marquis possessed several which were very like those that had been stolen from her.

She sent up a little prayer that one day they might come back.

Because she was so intent on what she was doing she started when she heard a voice say:

"I feel, Miss Lang, you are trying to decide whether your collection is better than mine."

It was the Marquis, and she had not heard the Gentlemen join the Ladies.

"I am sure yours are older and more valuable," she answered, "but I like mine best."

The Marquis laughed.

"That is exactly the right answer, and I shall be interested to see what you think of my Picture Gallery."

"I want to see everything," Gina said, "and I am sure you have a well-stocked Library."

The Marquis laughed again.

"Could I have anything else? And I know how shocked you would be if I said I was not an ardent reader."

"I am sure that is what you are," Gina said seriously, "just as I was sure when I first saw you that you were an exceptional rider."

"I suppose," the Marquis said slowly, "you are telling me that you use your instinct, as I do, rather than accept the obvious."

"It is what I have been able to do since I was very small," Gina replied, "and I am seldom mistaken."

"Then we will both be able to work hard in the same direction," the Marquis said.

He left her then to talk to his other guests.

Gina saw Lady Imogen move towards him, attempting to hold his attention so that everybody could see how close they were to each other.

"I do not like her," Gina told herself. "There is something wrong, though I am not sure what it is."

They were the same words she had used about Captain Dawes, and she looked round to see what he was doing.

To her delight she saw that the Gentleman who had sat on her Mother's right at dinner was again beside her and was holding her attention.

She had been introduced to him when she arrived and she knew he was the Marquis's Uncle, Lord William Lake.

He was a distinguished looking man.

She had watched her Mother during dinner

and had known that whatever he was saying to her had been pleasant because she had been smiling.

She had been attending to him, without apparently, while Gina was watching her, looking to where Guy Dawes was sitting.

He was struggling to obtain her attention now, but not being very successful.

'It would be marvelous,' Gina thought, 'if there were other men in Mama's life. I am sure it is only because she has been so lonely and Captain Dawes was so persistent that she has spent so much time with him.'

She looked at him and thought his face was rather flushed. He had obviously drunk a great deal of the fine wines that had been served at dinner.

And yet he seemed very sure of himself, and she wondered despairingly what the Marquis could do to make him leave her Mother alone.

"He will never do that as long as there is any money left," she told herself.

Card-tables were being arranged in the next room and there was also a game which any number of people could play.

Some of the Ladies found this amusing.

Some of the Gentlemen sat down to gamble.

"To-morrow," Gina heard the Marquis announce, "I have arranged for us to dance, but to-night I thought you would be tired after the journey and wish to go to bed early."

"I think that is a very sensible idea, Hengis,"

one of the Ladies said.

She said it in a provocative manner which did not sound as if she wished to rest.

Gina noticed that she put out her hand and laid it on the arm of a good-looking man called Harry, who she gathered was a close friend of the Marquis's.

Most of the women seemed to be paired off with a man.

Her Mother was still talking to Lord William and Gina thought a little wistfully that she herself was the odd one out.

It was then the Marquis unexpectedly came to her side.

"I have an idea, Miss Lang," he said, "that you would like to ride to-morrow morning."

Gina's eyes lit up.

"You know it is something I should very much enjoy."

"Most of my guests will be riding about noon when we will have some races before luncheon, and after luncheon, several more. But I am riding at seven o'clock, if that is not too early for you."

"I will not keep you waiting," Gina said, "and thank you for thinking of me."

As soon as he had finished speaking she slipped away upstairs and went to bed.

She thought of asking her Mother to come too, then thought it was a mistake as she was still talking to Lord William.

As she got into bed she thought that the Marquis was the kindest man she had ever met.

'I am sure his horses will be as fine as he is,' was her last thought before she fell asleep.

The Ladies gradually left the Drawing-Room saying that they were tired and wanted to retire early.

Some of the men were only too glad to do the same thing.

Finally the Marquis found that there were only four men still in the Salon besides himself.

They were playing Pontoon and gambling high on the turn of the cards.

He poured himself out a glass of lemonade from a jug on the table in the corner.

He never drank a lot if he was riding the next morning.

He intended to enjoy the races he had arranged for his guests in the afternoon.

And of course to display the spectacular skill of his horses over the jumps.

With the glass of lemonade in his hand he wandered over to the card-table where the players were too intent on their gambling to notice him.

As the Marquis reached the table Guy Dawes had his back to him.

The Marquis heard the player on the other side of the table call out a bet.

As he did so he saw Guy Dawes move his hand swiftly and cheat.

For a moment, because he was so surprised that such a thing should happen in his own house, the Marquis could not believe what he had seen.

He heard Guy Dawes accept the bet, and he won because he had changed a card.

It was then that the Marquis deliberately let his glass of lemonade fall on the table splashing over all the cards and making all four men stop.

"I am sorry — forgive me!" he said. "I cannot imagine how I could have been so clumsy."

He took his handkerchief from his pocket and started to dab the cards which were wet, saying as he did so:

"I am afraid that hand is null and void, and I can only apologise profusely for spoiling your game."

The man who had called out a bet rose to his feet.

"It is getting late," he said, "and we have had a long day. I think I shall leave things as they are until to-morrow."

"That is a very good idea," another man said.

"What I think you had better all do," the Marquis intervened, "is to cancel your bets and start again fresh. There is not only to-morrow, but also Sunday and Monday during which you can empty your pockets."

"Dammit all, Mortlake, I won!" one man protested.

"And doubtless these sharks will take it off you to-morrow," the Marquis joked.

He offered them a drink, but they refused, saying:

"Your wine is always superb, Hengis, and that was the best dinner I have ever had, except for the one we ate last time I was here."

"I must tell my Chef," the Marquis said. "He gets very frustrated and depressed if he does not receive any praise for what he produces."

They had reached the Hall.

Just as they were going up the stairs the Marquis said:

"Oh, just a minute, Dawes, I have something to show you. Will you come into my Study?"

Guy Dawes looked surprised.

At the same time, he thought he was being singled out as a favour and he obligingly followed the Marquis into his Study.

The Marquis closed the door and walked over to the fire-place saying:

"I saw you cheating just now, which is why I stopped the game. You now have a choice to make and I will tell you what it is."

Guy Dawes went very pale.

Then he stammered:

"I do not know . . . what you are talking about."

"You know perfectly well," the Marquis answered. "You cheated over that last hand, and I also consider it to be cheating when a man who is supposed to be a Gentleman takes money from a much older woman with no husband to protect her."

"I . . . I do not think that is . . . any of your business," Guy Dawes blustered.

The Marquis held up his hand.

"That you are an Officer in my Regiment makes your behaviour very much my business. These two matters alone could have you drummed out of the Regiment."

Guy Dawes went paler than before.

As if he felt his legs could no longer support him he sat down in one of the chairs and put his head in his hands.

"What can I do?" he asked in a broken voice. "What can I do?"

"I told you you have a choice," the Marquis answered, "so listen attentively. I can go to your Commanding Officer, tell him what has occurred and, as I have said, have you dismissed ignominiously from the Regiment."

He paused before he went on:

"Unfortunately that would cause a scandal which would certainly distress those who have served with you and believe themselves to be your friends."

"They will kill me!" Guy Dawes muttered.

"I would not blame them if they did," the Marquis said. "At the same time I am very proud of my Regiment, and what you have done would affect us all and besmirch its good name."

"Save me . . . please save me," Guy Dawes begged.

There was a glimmer of hope in what the Marquis knew were stricken eyes.

"The alternative to what I have just told you," the Marquis replied, "is that you return to London immediately and ask your Commanding Officer to send you abroad to fight with Wellington's Army. He will not refuse, for you will be carrying with you a letter from me saying it is of the greatest importance, for reasons which I will discuss with him later, that you should sail with the next shipment of reinforcements, which I happen to know are leaving England next week."

"You will tell the Colonel . . . why I have to go?" Guy Dawes questioned.

"I will make it clear to him that I will give him excellent reasons for my request when I next see him, which will be after you have left."

Guy Dawes drew in his breath.

"Does he . . . have to know, My Lord?" he asked piteously.

"He will know, but nobody else will," the Marquis answered. "I am disgusted by your behaviour, for which there is no excuse for a man who is supposed to be a Gentleman!"

His voice was sharp as if he was using a whip, and Guy Dawes once again put his hands over his face.

The Marquis went to his desk.

"It is a moonlit night," he said, "and I will arrange for your phaeton to be brought round at once. I will make your excuses to Lady Langdale to-morrow."

"You will not tell her about me?" Guy Dawes added. "It would cause her great distress."

"I shall not tell her for that very reason," the

117

Marquis replied, "and not because I wish to save you!"

There was silence while he wrote the letter.

Then as he sealed it he said:

"Incidentally, where did you sell the snuff-boxes which you stole from Lord Langdale's collection?"

Guy Dawes raised his head from his hands to stare at the Marquis.

"How can — you know about — that?" he muttered.

"I want an answer," the Marquis said.

"I sold them to Rubens in Covent Garden."

The Marquis wrote the name down on a pad and said:

"For that reason, if for no other, you could be sent to prison. If you do return eventually to England, remember that you are not a very skilful thief. Otherwise you will end up on the gallows."

The Marquis rose from the desk and walked back to where Guy Dawes was sitting.

"Here is the letter," he said coldly. "Do not try to cheat me, or I will have you arrested and taken before the Magistrates for theft, if for nothing else."

"I will do as you say," Guy Dawes muttered.

"You will do exactly as I say," the Marquis repeated firmly. "You will say good-bye to no one, not even your family. You will in fact just disappear and any questions will be answered by me."

"I . . . I do not know what to . . . say," Guy Dawes said unhappily.

118

"There is nothing to say," the Marquis retorted. "You have cheated at cards, which alone would ensure your being turned out of the Regiment, out of White's, and out of any other Club of which you are a member."

He saw the stricken look in Dawes's eyes and went on:

"You have taken large sums of money from a widow, which is not the behaviour of a Gentleman, and you have stolen a number of valuable objects from her house when she trusted you as a friend."

His voice sharpened as he finished:

"In my opinion, you are utterly and completely despicable, and I am only saving you to spare my Regiment from being humiliated by your behaviour becoming known."

The Marquis did not wait for Guy Dawes to answer but said as if he was giving an order to a new recruit:

"Go and pack your belongings and leave as quickly as possible. I hope this will be the last I shall ever see or hear of you."

As he finished speaking the Marquis walked over to the door and opened it.

Guy Dawes went out with shoulders sagging and his head down.

The Marquis closed the door and walked across the room to the window.

He pulled back the curtains.

There was a half-moon, but the stars were very bright in the sky.

He thought over what had happened and could not help feeling that luck had been on his side and on Gina's.

He had disposed of an unpleasant young man who might easily lose his life in one of the battles that lay ahead.

Alternately, the Army could save him from himself.

No man could go through the horrors of war and remain untouched.

Outside the scene was an enchantment.

The light from above made it seem as if it had nothing to do with the frailties of the human race.

The Marquis stood looking out for a long time.

Then as he turned away he thought that Gina would be very grateful.

She would undoubtedly think him even more wonderful than she did already.

"It was just Fate that I should have caught him cheating at cards," the Marquis told himself. "Quite obviously at this moment Fate is on my side."

As he walked up the stairs the footmen behind him started dimming some of the lights and he remembered that Imogen would be waiting for him.

Then he knew forcefully and unmistakably that while he might have solved Gina's problem, he was left with one of his own.

chapter six

Gina reached the stable-yard at five minutes to seven the next morning to find that the Marquis was already there.

Her eyes lit up when she saw him.

Then she realised that he was not alone.

Harry Vivian was with him and, although she did not quite know why, she felt a pang of disappointment.

"Good morning!" the Marquis said. "You are very punctual, which I find commendable in any woman!"

Gina laughed.

"If ever I was late for my Father, he treated me as if I were a raw recruit, and that was the worst punishment I could think of!"

"Now come and choose the horse you want to ride," the Marquis suggested.

He went into the stables, and Gina found that each horse was finer than the last.

It made it impossible to decide which one she wanted.

Finally she chose what she thought was a very spirited looking animal.

The Marquis approved her choice.

When all three were mounted, the Marquis led them from the stables towards the Race-Course which was to be used later in the day.

Gina was very impressed by the way in which it had been laid out.

The jumps were moveable and were all very high.

When the Marquis saw her looking at them he said:

"Those are for men only. You will ride in the flat races and I hope some of my other lady-guests will do the same."

Gina did not argue.

At the same time she hoped she would have a chance to try the jumps.

She knew she could manage them on the Marquis's horse.

He was trying out a new horse he had just bought and so was Harry.

The Marquis arranged a race in which he said Gina was to take part and he and Harry gave her a long start.

To her delight, although the Marquis won by a nose, she came in second and Harry was third.

"The trouble is," Harry said in a disgruntled voice, "you ride too well for a woman."

Gina laughed.

"I think the truth is that I was taught by my Father to ride like a man. He had no son and so I had to do all the things he would have expected of a son, including taking very high jumps."

She glanced at the Marquis as she spoke and he said:

"I know exactly what you are saying to me and I will think about it. In the meantime, we will have one of the highest put up and see how Harry manages it."

He told the men who were waiting for orders to arrange two jumps, one after the other.

They quickly obeyed him and put the jumps into place.

"Now, Harry," the Marquis said, "let us see how you fare, then I will follow you."

He moved to the side as Harry took his horse a long way back from the jumps.

When he was out of earshot the Marquis said to Gina:

"I have something to tell you."

"What is it?" Gina asked a little nervously.

"Dawes left last night and it is unlikely you will ever see him again."

Gina stared at the Marquis as if she could not believe what she had heard.

After a long silence she said:

"How can . . . you have . . . managed that? What . . . happened?"

"I arranged for him to go back to London," the Marquis explained. "He is to rejoin his Regiment and leave in a troop-ship which I know is sailing from Tilbury early on Wednesday morning."

"And . . . he agreed?" Gina asked breathlessly.

"He had no choice," the Marquis said grimly.

For a moment it was impossible for Gina to speak.

Then she said:

"How can I . . . thank you for being . . . so kind?"

"I also extracted from Dawes the information as to where he sold your Father's snuff-boxes," the Marquis went on. "I am sending a man to London to-morrow so that he can be at the shop first thing on Monday morning and buy them back for you."

Because it was such a surprise and also such a relief, Gina could only look at him.

It was impossible to express what she felt.

The Marquis smiled at her.

Then as if he was embarrassed by her gratitude he turned to where Harry was jumping over the fence.

Horse and rider managed it magnificently.

As he landed safely the Marquis shouted: "Bravo!" and rode forward.

Gina could only follow him, thinking that what he had just told her was incredible and she must be dreaming.

As Harry pulled in his horse the Marquis said in a low voice:

"Do not repeat a word of what I have told you to anyone, including your Mother. I will tell Lady Langdale and the rest of the party that Dawes had to return to his Regiment and we need not speak of him again."

"You know . . . what I want to say," Gina said in a low voice.

"I will take it for granted," the Marquis answered, "and if you obey me as I wish you to do, I will allow you to try to jump this fence."

She flashed him a smile before she rode quickly back to the point where Harry had started with his horse.

As she sailed over the jump in the same way that he had, Harry clapped his hands.

"Magnificent!" he enthused. "But you nearly gave me a heart attack thinking you could not manage it."

"I am glad to have proved you wrong," Gina said.

Harry went on praising her, but she was looking at the Marquis.

She felt, although he did not say so, that he was delighted that she had proved herself.

It was in fact the highest jump she had ever attempted.

They rode until breakfast-time, then returned to the house.

There were several other men in the Breakfast-Room, but no Ladies.

"You might have asked us to join you, Hengis," one of the men said. "Your stable is so fine that I would have made the effort."

"There will be plenty of time for you to ride later in the day," the Marquis replied. "I have arranged a number of races to start about eleven o'clock, then again after luncheon you can try the jumps from which the Ladies are excluded."

He glanced at Gina as he spoke.

She knew he did not wish to say that she had been jumping this morning.

While the men were still eating, Gina went upstairs to change.

As she came from her bedroom a little later she saw Lady Imogen coming down the passage.

"Good-morning, Miss Lang," she said. "I see you are an early riser like myself, but I do not expect the other Ladies in the party to join us for at least an hour."

Gina realised that Lady Imogen thought she had just got up.

It occurred to her that she might be jealous if she thought she had been out early riding with the Marquis.

"Of course it is ridiculous for her to be jealous of anybody, considering how close they are," she told herself.

She once again felt that strange little pang in her breast.

It was what she had experienced when she had gone to the stables and found Harry Vivian there with the Marquis.

Downstairs the men were all congregating in the Hall before moving towards the stables.

Gina had changed into another habit.

It was smarter and more elegant than the one she had worn earlier.

Her riding-hat was in the latest fashion with a high crown encircled with a gauze veil which hung down her back.

Because it was the latest fashion, Lady Imogen was dressed in very much the same way.

Her habit was dark red trimmed with white braid.

It certainly became her dark colouring.

The male guests were clustering round her.

It made Gina suddenly feel somewhat insignificant.

'I do not really belong with women like Lady Imogen,' she thought. 'When I return to London I do not suppose the Marquis will ever invite me again, or even wish to see me.'

The sun seemed to have gone behind a cloud.

It was well after eleven o'clock before everybody was assembled.

Then there was the difficulty of mounting the other Lady-guests.

Two of the older women, however, wished only to watch.

The Marquis chose the horses.

He did not listen when they told him what they wanted, which was invariably a horse that was well-trained and not too difficult to handle.

Gina found she was given an even more spirited horse than the one she had ridden in the morning.

Although the Marquis did not say anything, she knew it was a compliment.

There were several races in which the Ladies were given a long start.

To Gina's delight she won one.

But after that she was handicapped by the Marquis so that she did not win any snore.

When they went back to luncheon everybody was in very good spirits.

With the exception of Lady Imogen who, Gina knew, was angry with her because she had been so successful.

She showed her displeasure by seating her at luncheon between two of the older male guests.

She was even more angry when they both found Gina extremely interesting.

They discussed Politics as well as horses.

Gina was happy with the news the Marquis had given her, however.

She paid little attention to Lady Imogen's angry looks and the sharp, slightly insulting remarks she said to her.

What pleased her more than anything was that her Mother had been talking to Lord William when he was not competing in a race.

It was not until they went upstairs after luncheon to tidy themselves that Lady Langdale asked:

"What has happened to dear Guy? I have not seen him this morning."

"He has left, Mama," Gina replied.

"Left?" her mother repeated.

"He was recalled to his Regiment."

Lady Langdale was silent for a moment. Then she said:

"I do hope they will not send the dear boy out to Portugal. He would hate the discomfort and the rough way that we hear the troops are living. I am sure that he has no wish to kill anybody, not even a Frenchman!"

"He had to go, Mama," Gina said. "You would not have him disobey orders."

"No, of course not," Lady Langdale agreed. "But Lord William was telling me that the War Office thinks we are on the verge of victory, which is wonderful!"

"It certainly is, Mama," Gina agreed, "and do get Lord William to tell you about his career in the Army. I believe when he was a young man he was very adventurous."

She had heard this from the Marquis.

She had the idea he was telling her about his Uncle because he thought it would interest her Mother.

Gina was relieved that Lady Langdale was taking Guy Dawes's disappearance so mildly.

She only hoped that when they went back to London her mother would not be lonely without him.

"I wonder," she pondered, "if I could ask the Marquis to introduce her to some older men like his Uncle?"

Then she thought she could not impose on him any more when he had been so kind already.

The day passed quickly.

The jumps in the afternoon which had been put up on the Race-Course were a tremendous test of skill.

As there were no falls or injuries it was a very

satisfied party that returned to the house.

There was tea or champagne for the guests.

Afterwards the Ladies retired upstairs to rest before dinner.

Gina was not tired because everything was so exciting.

She therefore made her way to the Picture Gallery which she had not yet had a chance to visit.

As she expected the portraits were superb.

She spent a long time looking at them and was just leaving when the Marquis came into the Gallery.

"I heard you were here," he said, "but I had thought you were lying down."

"I was frightened of missing anything before we have to leave on Monday morning," Gina said, "I hope you do not mind?"

"Of course not!" the Marquis said. "And I am interested to hear what you have to say about my collection."

"Once again I have run out of adjectives," Gina answered. "I can only say that, like their owner, they are wonderful!"

She said it quite simply without making it sound in the least flirtatious.

The Marquis thought it was one of the most sincere compliments he had ever been paid.

"Thank you," he said, "but I do want you to admire a Botticelli which I bought many years ago when I was in Florence."

He walked towards the picture as he spoke and

Gina followed him.

It was one she had already been looking at for a long time.

Now when she reached it she said:

"It is so beautiful . . . so romantic . . . and at the same time it has a spiritual quality which one does not always find in such pictures."

"I think," the Marquis said slowly, "that it might be a portrait of you!"

Gina laughed.

"Now you are flattering me!" she said. "But I am very, very honoured to think that I might, in any way, resemble anything so exquisitely painted."

"And so exquisitely lovely!" the Marquis added.

"Now you are making me feel shy," Gina said. "I think perhaps I should . . . go and dress for dinner . . . otherwise I will be late and you will be . . . angry."

The Marquis did not reply.

He merely pointed out another picture that was by Poussin.

It surprised him that Gina should know so much about the artist.

In fact they delayed for so long in reaching the end of the Gallery that when they did so Gina said:

"Now I really will have to hurry, and if I am late in coming downstairs you will have to forgive me."

She smiled at him as she spoke, then ran away in the direction of her bedroom.

She moved so swiftly and at the same time with such grace that her feet seemed hardly to touch the ground.

"She is certainly unusual," the Marquis said to himself before he went to his own Master Suite.

It was in the same corridor in which Gina's bedroom was situated and also that of Lady Imogen.

As the Marquis opened the door of his room, where his Valet was waiting for him, Lady Imogen came out of her room.

"Good gracious, Hengis," she said, "you are not yet changed! You will have to hurry!"

"I realise that," the Marquis replied.

"Where have you been?" Lady Imogen enquired. "You left the Drawing-Room a long time ago and when I looked in your Study you were not there."

"I had various things to attend to," the Marquis answered.

He went into his bedroom and shut the door behind him.

As he did so he thought it extremely annoying that Imogen should watch his every move.

Being conscious of it, he felt compelled to try to avoid her scrutiny.

As he started to undress, his Valet noted that he was frowning and wondered what had upset him.

A number of neighbours came to dinner that evening.

As the Marquis had promised, there was a small Orchestra to play for them in the Ball-Room.

It was one of the prettiest rooms Gina had ever seen.

There were long windows opening out into the garden.

Just outside the Marquis had arranged for Chinese lanterns to be suspended from the branches of the trees.

There were also fairy-lights along the edges of the lawn.

Harry danced with Gina first and said:

"I know you are enjoying yourself. Is this the first Ball you have attended since you left School?"

"Mama took me to one in London after I returned, but this is far more exciting because it is in the country."

"Do you prefer the country?" Harry asked.

"Of course!" Gina replied. "Especially when there are horses like those I was riding to-day."

"You ride superbly!" Harry said. "You made the other women look like bags of suet."

"Oh, I hope not!" Gina exclaimed in dismay. "I do not want anybody to think I can beat them to the winning-post. It always makes for unhappiness."

She thought as she spoke of how jealous the girls at School had been when she won so many prizes.

She found at dinner that, just as at luncheon,

Lady Imogen was giving her angry glances.

'I am not interfering with her,' Gina thought, 'so why should she trouble about me?'

She did not lack for partners, but the Marquis did not ask her to dance.

In a way she was relieved because she was certain it would annoy Lady Imogen.

After a very dreamy waltz which she had danced with Harry she stepped out into the garden.

She did not have a partner for the next dance.

She moved across the lawn.

Once out of the light of the Chinese lanterns she was aware that the stars were twinkling like diamonds in the sky.

There was a young moon moving up towards them.

As she walked on a little further she had a view of the sea.

In the light coming from the sky it was very beautiful.

Without thinking, Gina walked farther away from the house.

Finally she could no longer hear the Orchestra playing, but only the sounds of the night.

There was the rustle of small animals beneath the trees.

A bird fluttered off a branch at her approach.

As she went farther she could hear the waves breaking on the rocks.

It was so lovely, so magical, that she forgot everything but the beauty of it and walked on.

At last she came to what she saw was an inlet with a small stream flowing into it.

From this point the ground sloped down steeply to a little beach.

When she left the garden, she had walked along the side of a wood lined with clumps of bushes.

To take a little rest, she sat down on the edge of the slope beside the last of the bushes.

She was looking at the sea and the light of the stars reflected in it.

Suddenly, below where she was sitting, she heard footsteps.

She looked down and saw to her astonishment there was a man walking along what she supposed was a path at the side of the stream.

He was carrying a barrel on his shoulder.

She could not see him at all clearly.

He was in the shadow of the higher ground on which she was sitting.

As he drew nearer she saw there was another man, and yet another behind him.

She drew in her breath, realising that they were smugglers.

They must have left their boat just inside the cove.

They were now moving the goods they had brought over from France up to some hiding-place.

It struck her how angry the Marquis would be if he knew what was happening on his land.

She wondered if she should tell him.

While she was debating this she suddenly heard

a voice quite near to her.

It came from the other side of the bushes.

"You are earlier than I expected!"

It was a woman's voice and Gina thought it sounded familiar.

Then she heard a man reply:

"The sea is as calm as a mill-pond, and I have brought back a better consignment than we have ever had before. I was only afraid you might not be here."

He spoke in an educated manner, but there was just a touch of an accent in his voice.

It made Gina think he was not completely English.

The woman replied:

"That is good! I have been able to meet you as arranged because I am staying at Arrowhead."

Gina stiffened.

She knew now, without a shadow of a doubt, that the woman speaking was Lady Imogen.

"I thought Your Ladyship would manage it somehow," the man replied.

"And you saw General Richelieu?" Lady Imogen enquired.

"I did, and he was very grateful for the information you gave him about the reinforcements sailing to join the Duke of Wellington."

"I thought he would be," Lady Imogen replied.

"Here is your money he has sent you," the man went on.

Lady Imogen did not speak.

Gina however felt sure she was taking something from the man's hands and thought it would be a bag containing gold.

The gold she was being paid for the information she had given to the French.

Gina could hardly grasp the enormity of it.

Then she heard Lady Imogen ask:

"Did you bring me what else I asked for?"

"I have it here," the man replied, "but the General says it is very potent. Three drops in a glass of wine will render the person who drinks it completely your slave, obeying everything you ask of him for about twenty-four hours."

"Good!" Lady Imogen exclaimed. "I know how to use it, and it is exactly what I want."

"I am glad Your Ladyship is pleased," the man remarked.

"I have expressed my pleasure in what I have transcribed on this Note of Hand," Lady Imogen said, "and thank you, thank you very much."

"It is always a pleasure to deal with Your Ladyship," the man replied, "and I will let you know the price we obtain for the cargo and the day of our next crossing. It will take me a little time to dispose of this consignment, seeing how large it is."

"The larger the better!" Lady Imogen replied.

She gave a little laugh as she spoke.

Gina was suddenly aware of the implications of what she had just overheard.

She knew, as if somebody was explicitly telling her so, why Lady Imogen required the drug that had been brought to her from France.

There was no doubt on whom she intended to use it.

She was frightened, not only for the Marquis, but also in case she might be discovered.

Very carefully she rose from where she was sitting.

Slowly, moving so that she would not be heard, she edged herself away.

She moved back through the bushes.

She was well aware that on no account must Lady Imogen see her.

If she did, she would somehow contrive to prevent her from reaching the Marquis, even if it meant killing her.

She knew without being told that a woman who could betray her country for money would not shrink from murder if it was in her own interests.

'I have to get back . . . I have to!' Gina thought.

She did not stand upright, but moved in a crouching position.

She kept to the undergrowth just in case she should be seen by anybody moving behind her.

When she thought it was safe she ran between the trees.

Finally, after what seemed to her a very long time, she reached the bottom of the garden.

Now she could hear again the music of the Orchestra and it was somehow comforting.

The guests would still be dancing.

The Marquis would have no idea of what had been happening outside.

Nor would he guess the horror of what was waiting for him.

Gina forced herself to walk slowly back towards the fairy lights and the Chinese lanterns.

As she reached them she was aware that two men were standing just outside the Ball-Room windows.

They were the Marquis and Harry Vivian talking to each other.

With a supreme effort Gina prevented herself from running across the lawn and flinging herself against the Marquis.

Instead she walked sedately up to them feeling as if every footstep she took was weighted down.

"There you are!" the Marquis exclaimed. "I wondered why you had disappeared."

"I wanted to look at the sea," Gina said. "It was so lovely."

She thought her tone of voice sounded unnatural, but the two men did not seem to notice it.

"Just as you are!" Harry said gallantly. "Are you going to dance with me again?"

"I think it is my turn," the Marquis interposed, "and the Orchestra is playing a tune I particularly like."

"Then of course I must allow you to take precedence over me," Harry joked. "It is something I seem to have been doing continually all my life."

"If you are complaining, you can of course find a more congenial place to stay!" the Marquis retorted.

They were teasing each other as they always did.

As they laughed, Gina tried to laugh too.

She felt however as if every nerve in her body was tense.

Even as the Marquis led her through the windows and onto the Dance-Floor she saw Lady Imogen come into the room through one of the doors.

Gina knew she must have approached the house from a different direction.

As she looked at Lady Imogen their eyes met.

Gina was aware that the older woman was furious because she was dancing with the Marquis.

Frightened that she might interrupt and somehow contrive to take the Marquis away, Gina said in a whisper:

"I have to . . . speak to you . . . alone! It is very . . . important!"

The Marquis looked surprised.

However he replied:

"That will be easy, and as soon as the dance ends we can go back into the garden."

"I have to speak to . . . you before Lady Imogen . . . does!" Gina said urgently.

As she spoke she had the terrifying feeling that somehow Lady Imogen would get the Marquis to drink the drug before she had a chance to warn him.

From the way the Marquis held her fingers more tightly, she knew that he was surprised at

140

the urgency with which she spoke.

As the dance came to an end he walked with her out of the Ball-Room.

Without speaking he moved quickly along the corridors.

They reached his Study.

He opened the door and as Gina slipped through it he said:

"Now, what is all this about? I can tell you are frightened."

"I am . . . very . . . very . . . frightened," Gina admitted.

They were just inside the Study.

The Marquis stopped and turned the key in the lock.

"Now," he said, "we shall not be disturbed and you can tell me what has frightened you."

Gina hesitated a moment.

It suddenly struck her that perhaps he would not believe her.

It would not be surprising considering that even to herself what she had overheard seemed so unbelievable.

In fact so far-fetched that anyone would question it.

The Marquis walked to the grog-tray.

"I am going to give you a glass of champagne," he said. "I can see that something has upset you but, whatever it is, I promise I will put it right."

"No . . . no . . . please . . . I want . . . nothing," Gina said, "except to tell you what I have . . . overheard and to . . . warn you."

"Warn me?" the Marquis said. "About what?"

He was obviously astonished and Gina said:

"Just now, because the stars were shining so brightly and . . . everything looked so beautiful . . . I went for a walk towards the sea."

The Marquis said, "I saw you were not in the Ball-Room."

"I was not really . . . thinking about anything . . . except the loveliness of the night . . . until I came to the cove."

"What happened?" the Marquis asked.

"I saw some . . . men coming up . . . from the shore."

The Marquis stiffened.

"Smugglers I suppose," he said grimly. "I have told the village before now that I will not have them taking part in this dastardly trade. It gives Bonaparte the money he requires to buy arms and ammunition with which to kill our men."

Before Gina could speak he went on:

"You are quite certain of what you saw? I will challenge the Ring-Leader whom I know quite well and stop this abominable trade from taking place again."

"I am quite . . . certain of what I saw," Gina replied, "but . . . there is much more to it than that."

The Marquis looked at her in surprise.

Then he said:

"Tell me everything that happened."

"That is what I am . . . going to do," Gina said, "but . . . I am afraid it will . . . upset you.

I was so frightened that I hurried back to be in time to . . . warn you."

"Warn me of what?" the Marquis asked. "Who has frightened you?"

Because she suddenly felt that what she had to say was very embarrassing, Gina looked away from him.

"It was . . . Lady Imogen," she said, "she was . . . talking to a man who had brought her . . . money in return for information she had passed on to a General Richelieu."

The Marquis stared at her.

Then he moved to the sofa and took her hand in his.

"Tell me everything," he said, "and do not be afraid. No one can overhear us here, and anyway I will protect you."

Without meaning to, Gina's fingers clung to his.

Then she told him everything she had heard while sheltering behind the bushes.

chapter seven

The Marquis walked across the passage and into Imogen's bedroom.

He had undressed and was wearing the long robe which was frogged across the front and made him look very military.

Lady Imogen was not in bed as he expected.

Instead she was reclining on the sofa in a very diaphanous négligée.

He knew her pose was intended to excite him.

With an effort he forced himself to appear at his ease.

There was, he saw, a bottle of champagne and two glasses on a table near the sofa.

"I am glad you sent everybody away early," Lady Imogen said.

"I thought it correct as it is now Sunday," the Marquis answered, "but because they were enjoying the party our neighbours were reluctant to go."

"Of course they were," Lady Imogen replied. "Who could fail to enjoy any party you gave?"

"That is what I like to think," the Marquis answered. "At the same time, it is always slightly worrying when one entertains."

"Not when I am there to help you," Lady Imogen said softly. "I know you must be pleased that our guests enjoyed themselves so much and everything has gone so smoothly."

"Of course I am," the Marquis agreed.

"What I thought we would do," Lady Imogen went on, "is to drink a toast, dearest Hengis, to our happiness. That is why I asked for a bottle of champagne, and I am going to pour us each a glass with which we can toast one another."

The Marquis realised where all this was leading, but he merely said:

"Very well, of course I will do what you want, and you shall propose the toast."

Lady Imogen moved her legs from the sofa and sat up so that she could pour out the champagne.

As she poured it the Marquis walked across the room to the dressing-table.

He stood in front of the mirror smoothing back his hair.

He could just see, without appearing to do so, what Imogen was doing.

He saw her fill two glasses, then put a few drops from a small bottle into the glass furthest from her.

He knew then that Gina had not been mistaken in saying that the man to whom Lady Imogen was talking had brought a drug from France.

The Marquis knew who the man was.

He was in fact the School-Master in the village.

He had French blood in him but, because he

was an educated man and the School children had learnt a lot from him, the Marquis had not sacked him.

That was what had happened to most French people in England when war had recommenced after the short Armistice.

Now he knew he had made a fatal mistake.

He was determined to have the man removed and the smugglers stopped.

The villagers would return to the quiet existence which they had enjoyed in the past.

He blamed himself now for being so lax in not realising the smuggling was going on.

He was furious to think that it had been encouraged by Imogen.

But what was much more serious was that she had received money from the French for information she had sent across the Channel.

All the time he was undressing he had been wondering if he personally had said to her anything which might have been useful to Bonaparte.

It was terrifying to fear that in some unwary moment he had given her information which had meant the death of one of his own countrymen.

He was watching her while he was apparently concerned with his own reflection.

As he did so he saw her put into the glass several more drops from the small bottle.

If Gina was right, then the moment he drank it he would become completely subservient to anything Imogen required.

He knew only too well what that was.

He would, on her insistence, ask her to marry him.

He was only surprised that she had not arranged to have a Marriage Service in the Chapel.

Perhaps that was to come immediately after.

She could give him a second dose of the drug if he was not as acquiescent as he should be.

The whole idea appalled him.

His impulse was to turn round, accuse her, and tell her he never wished to see or speak to her again.

He was about to do this when he suddenly remembered something.

If he did send Imogen away there were a great many other men who would succumb to her beauty.

With her exotic attractiveness she would make them divulge more information for which she would be paid by the French.

After the years of fighting in Wellington's Army, the Marquis knew only too well how dangerous an English informer could be.

It meant that Napoleon would be aware of what was being planned.

How many troops were being sent out from England.

He thought of the courage and endurance of the men who had fought at his side.

It told him exactly where his loyalty lay.

He was just about to turn round when he saw Imogen once again shaking the bottle she had received from France over his glass.

He guessed she had decided that twenty-four hours was not long enough to ensure that she became his wife.

If he continued to be in a state of drugged subservience they could be married tomorrow, or the next day.

It would be a waste of time to risk his becoming normal again too quickly.

He might repudiate everything she had made him say under the influence of the drug.

He turned from the mirror saying:

"I am waiting for your toast and I think as it is such a lovely night we should draw back the curtains and drink while the stars overhead make us feel romantic."

Imogen smiled.

"You know, dearest Hengis," she said, "I always feel romantic with you, very, very romantic, and it is what I want you to feel with me."

As the Marquis made no move towards either of the windows in the room Imogen got up.

She went to the nearer one.

She drew back the curtains and opened the casements.

It was a warm night without a breath of wind.

The stars seemed to glitter in her green eyes as she looked out.

The Marquis, however, as she drew the curtains, had moved to the table by the sofa.

As she opened the casements he swiftly switched the glasses.

The one intended for him he placed where

Imogen's had been, and the other he lifted from the table.

He was standing with it in his hand when she turned, obviously expecting him to say something.

Somewhat mechanically he said:

"You look very beautiful with the stars haloing your head."

"And you look very handsome," she answered. "What could be a better beginning to an unforgettable night than that we should toast each other with love?"

As she spoke she picked up the glass which had been intended for him.

With difficulty the Marquis repressed an impulse to tell her not to drink it.

Then he remembered from where it had come and his lips tightened.

Imogen raised her glass.

"To our happiness, my adorable Hengis, and may it last for ever!"

The Marquis raised his glass in response, but although he put it to his lips, he did not drink.

"No heel-taps!" Imogen exclaimed.

She threw back her head as she spoke and poured the champagne down her throat.

Then she gasped as if for breath.

She staggered and while the Marquis watched as if mesmerised she subsided slowly onto the floor.

The glass fell from her hand and as her head touched the carpet the Marquis could see that her eyes were closed.

She lay in a patch of silver moonlight coming through the window.

He put down his glass of champagne untouched.

Lady Imogen did not move.

He walked towards her thinking that the drug must be stronger than she had expected.

General Richelieu had obviously been right in saying she should use only a little of it for the effect she wanted.

Then, as he saw her lying very still, he had a sudden thought which was frightening.

Going down on one knee he put his hand first to her forehead, then to her pulse and finally to her heart.

General Richelieu had tricked Imogen.

He had deliberately, the Marquis realised, given her a drug which would not merely bemuse him but would kill him!

Gina passed a restless night.

She was worried about the Marquis, being desperately afraid that he would somehow be persuaded into drinking the drug.

And then he would lose his will-power.

She wondered if instead he would confront Lady Imogen before she attempted to use it.

It would, she thought, be a sensible thing to do.

"How could any woman want to capture a man in such a manner?" she asked.

150

Yet she could understand in a way that Lady Imogen was unscrupulous enough to attempt anything to get what she desired.

How was it possible for her not to desire the Marquis when he was so handsome, attractive and charming?

He was at the same time of great importance in the country as well as being very rich.

"Of course she loved him," Gina told herself.

She turned over and over against her pillow, wondering desperately if the Marquis was all right.

Then she knew that she too loved him.

It was love that had made her feel so happy because he had been kind to her.

It was love that had made her know that when he was in the room there was nobody else there.

It was love that was beating tempestuously in her breast now because she was afraid for him.

"I love him! I love him!" she murmured.

Then she knew he was as far out of her reach as the stars in the sky.

How could he ever think of her except as a young girl whom he was helping because he had known her Father?

As she thought of Lady Imogen's sinuous grace, the beauty of her face and her confidence in herself, Gina felt very young and ignorant.

"What do I know of the world in which she and the Marquis live?" she asked. "Why should I ever know anything about it?"

Then the tears ran down her cheeks and, hiding her face in the pillow, she cried.

She fell asleep just before dawn from sheer exhaustion.

Gina awoke when the maid came in to pull back the curtains.

Having let in the sunshine the maid came to her bed-side.

" 'Scuse me, Miss, but there's bin a tragedy in th' 'ouse last night."

"A . . . tragedy?" Gina asked.

She thought it must be the Marquis and felt the blood drain away from her cheeks.

Her whole body trembled.

"W-What has happened?" she asked in a whisper.

"T'was. 'Er Ladyship — Lady Imogen — died of a 'eart attack, Miss!" the maid replied. " 'Is Lordship's already left, takin' 'er body back to 'er own 'ome."

It was difficult for Gina to take in what the maid was saying.

Then as she realised that the Marquis was unharmed she felt her heart start to beat again.

"His Lordship . . . is all right?" she stammered.

"Ow, 'e's all right, Miss," the maid replied, "an' he left you this note before 'e left. Everyone's goin' away this mornin'. It's wot 'Is Lordship wished."

"They are all . . . going away?" Gina asked rather stupidly.

"Yes, Miss. We was all given our orders to

pack for th' Ladies an' carriages'll be round at eleven o'clock. Oi brought your breakfast up for you as I thinks you'd not want t' be downstairs with th' Gentlemen in th' Breakfast-Room."

"N-No . . . of course not!" Gina said quickly. "Thank you for bringing my breakfast up."

" 'Tis a terrible shock, that's wot it is," the maid said talkatively as she came in with Gina's breakfast on a tray, "just drops down dead in 'er room, 'Er Ladyship did — 'Is Lordship sent for th' Doctor, but there weren't nothin' 'e could do."

"You say it was a . . . heart attack?" Gina murmured.

"That's right, Miss. Took 'er off suddenlike. Before you knows it, 'er's dead!"

Gina thought the Marquis had been very clever.

She guessed that, in some way she could not fathom, Lady Imogen rather than he had taken the drug.

It had obviously not just paralysed the brain as she expected, but had killed Lady Imogen.

"No one will ever know the truth," she told herself, "and I must be very careful not to appear too curious."

At the same time it was an agony to be going away from Arrowhead without saying good-bye to the Marquis.

She joined the guests of the house-party in the Hall.

They were waiting for their trunks to be placed on the carriages outside.

They were all discussing Lady Imogen's sudden and tragic death and wondering how soon they would see the Marquis again.

But there was no reason to suppose, Gina thought, that he would trouble himself with her.

This was good-bye to Arrowhead and its owner.

She looked round the magnificent Hall and thought she would always remember the beauty of it.

The Butler announced the carriage in which she and her Mother were to travel was outside.

A few people said good-bye to them somewhat perfunctorily.

They were worrying about their own conveyances and disappointed that such an enjoyable visit had been cut short.

There was no sign of Harry Vivian.

Gina guessed he had gone with the Marquis to carry Lady Imogen's body back to Milchester Hall.

It was, she knew, about the same distance as they had to travel to reach the Marquis's half-way house.

They were to stay there the night before proceeding to London.

Gina noticed that her Mother was having an intimate talk with Lord William before she stepped into the carriage.

As the horses moved off and he waved them good-bye, Lady Langdale said:

"We will see Lord William again to-night. It will be delightful to have dinner with him."

She spoke in a satisfied manner which made

Gina realise she was not giving a thought to Guy Dawes.

"As you seem to like Lord William so much, Mama," she said, "I hope he will come to see us in London."

"You can be certain of that," Lady Langdale replied with a smile. "He is so charming and we have so much in common. I have asked him to luncheon the day after to-morrow."

The way she spoke made Gina look at her sharply.

Then she asked a little tentatively:

"Do you think . . . Mama . . . that Lord William is . . . in love with you?"

There was silence before Lady Langdale replied:

"It is too soon, Dearest, to be thinking of such things, but he is the most delightful man I have ever met, and he tells me he has been looking for me all his life."

"Oh, Mama, I am so glad for you and so very, very happy."

"And so am I," Lady Langdale replied. "But, as I have just said, it is too soon, and we must both get to know Lord William better before we make any hasty decisions."

Gina leaned back in the carriage feeling a sense of relief.

They were not only rid of Guy Dawes, but her Mother had a charming and ideal suitor.

She was quite sure she would eventually be very happy with him.

The carriage reached the end of the drive.

They turned onto the road leading through the village and Gina had a last view of Arrowhead.

The sunshine was glittering on the many windowpanes.

The house was silhouetted against the darkness of the trees behind it.

There were brilliant splashes of colour in the surrounding garden.

Gina thought nothing could be more lovely or more like a Palace in a Fairy Tale.

"And the Marquis is 'Prince Charming,' " she told herself, "and I shall never, never forget him."

As the horses drove on and the trees prevented her from seeing the house any longer she whispered in her heart:

"Good-bye."

They reached the Marquis's half-way house an hour before dinner.

Lady Langdale hurried upstairs to bathe and change into what she thought was one of her prettiest gowns.

As well as Lord William there were two other people staying with them in the house, but they had gone up to dress.

Gina was alone with Lord William.

He had arrived a little while before they did.

"I hope," he said in his courteous manner, "that your Mother is not too tired. I always think the only flaw I can find in Arrowhead is that it is so far from London."

"But so beautiful when you get there!" Gina murmured.

"I agree with you," Lord William answered. "It is very sad that the party should have to end on such a dismal note."

"It must have been very upsetting for the Marquis," Gina said quietly.

"Perhaps," Lord William agreed. "At the same time, I will be honest and admit that I have never liked Lady Imogen. She was a beautiful woman, but beauty is not all that one requires in a woman."

There was silence for a moment before he went on:

"Hengis is such a remarkable young man. I would like him to find a wife who is worthy of him and will make him happy. No man is completely happy if he lives alone."

He was thinking of himself, Gina guessed, and she said:

"Mama has enjoyed the visit enormously, and thank you for looking after her. She had been very lonely since my Father died."

There was silence until Lord William asked:

"Are you saying that you think your Mother should marry again?"

"I am praying that is what she will do," Gina replied. "She has never lived alone and she needs somebody to look after her."

She saw the light in Lord William's eyes.

Without saying any more, she went upstairs to dress.

Gina and her Mother reached their house in Berkeley Square the following afternoon and were both tired after the journey.

They had a light meal and went to bed.

"Do not forget," Gina said, "that Lord William is coming to luncheon to-morrow and you must look your best."

"Oh, Dearest, will you see to the luncheon?" Lady Langdale asked. "And ask Cook to make all her very best dishes."

"Just go to bed, Mama, and do not worry," Gina said. "I promise you Lord William will enjoy everything we give him."

She went to her own bedroom, but once again it was difficult to sleep.

She could only think of the Marquis having to explain to the Duke of Milchester what had happened to his daughter.

Perhaps he would have to stay on until after the Funeral Service.

She wondered if her thoughts of him winged out like birds across the long distance between them.

Then as she thought despairingly that she would never see him again the tears came.

She cried into her pillow until she was exhausted.

When finally she fell asleep she was murmuring over and over again:

"I love him . . . I love him . . . !"

Because Gina thought it tactful, she left her

Mother and Lord William alone before luncheon.

Having eaten with them, she then disappeared again.

She was sitting in her bedroom trying to read a book when her Mother came into the room.

"Hello, Mama," Gina said. "Has Lord William gone?"

"No, Dearest. I have just come to tell you that he is taking me to see the family house where he has been living ever since Hengis was sent to the Peninsula. It has a Greek statue which he says looks exactly like me!"

She smiled before she went on:

"After that we are going to have tea in his own house which has been shut up since the war began but which he wants to open again."

"With you as hostess, Mama?" Gina asked.

For a moment her Mother looked shy.

It made her even more beautiful than she was ordinarily.

"I think so . . . Dearest," she answered. "You would not . . . mind him . . . taking your Father's . . . place?"

"No, of course not, Mama," Gina said. "I just want you to be happy, looked after and protected, as you were by Papa."

Lady Langdale sighed.

"I am so lucky, so very lucky," she said, "not only to have met William, but also to have such an understanding daughter."

Gina kissed her.

"Go and get ready, Mama," she said. "No man

likes to be kept waiting."

"That is what your Father used to say," Lady Langdale replied, "and in some respects William is very like him."

Gina helped her Mother to put on her prettiest bonnet and her most attractive cloak.

When she had left, Gina went into the Drawing-Room.

The house seemed empty and she felt very much alone.

She stood by the window looking out into the small garden.

She was thinking of Arrowhead and the beauty of the flowers in the garden there.

She remembered the brilliance of the rhododendrons and the kingcups which surrounded the lake.

Because she could not help it the tears came into her eyes.

She wanted to cry because when she left Arrowhead, she had left her heart behind.

She heard the door open and thought it was a servant come to disturb her.

She did not turn round because her eyes were blinded with tears.

Then the door closed and she was aware that there was somebody in the room.

"What . . . is it?" she asked.

"I thought you might be glad to see me," a voice answered.

Gina swung round.

It was the Marquis!

He was there when she had least expected to see him.

It struck her that perhaps something had gone wrong and that was what he had come to tell her.

"W-What has . . . happened?" she asked and her voice was hardly above a whisper. "Is something . . . wrong? Are . . . people . . . suspicious?"

The questions seemed to tumble from between her lips.

The Marquis smiled as he walked towards her.

"Nothing is wrong," he replied. "I have come to thank you for saving my life."

"The Frenchman sent a . . . drug that was . . . intended to . . . kill . . . you?" Gina whispered.

The Marquis nodded.

"It would certainly have been a feather in his cap if, after I had recovered from a French bullet, he had been able to dispose of me."

"Supposing . . . he had . . . succeeded?" Gina gasped.

"He would have, if it had not been for you," the Marquis answered.

He had reached the window and was standing looking down at her.

"Why have you been crying?" he asked unexpectedly.

Gina hastily wiped her eyes.

It had so surprised her to see him that she had quite forgotten her tears.

"It is . . . all right now," she said. "I . . . I was just . . . worried."

"Because I thought that was how you might

be feeling," the Marquis said, "I came as soon as I could leave Milchester Hall."

Because he sounded concerned she looked up at him.

As their eyes met it was impossible for either of them to look away.

At last in a voice he could hardly hear Gina managed to say:

"You are . . . quite certain . . . everything is all . . . right?"

"It is, because I am alive, which I owe entirely to you."

"I . . . am glad, so very . . . very glad!" Gina murmured.

"That is what I want you to say," he answered, "but I wish to express my gratitude rather differently."

He bent forward as he spoke and put his arms round her.

She could hardly believe it was happening as he pulled her close to him.

Then as she looked up at him his lips came down on hers.

He kissed her as if she was infinitely precious.

As he felt the softness and innocence of her lips his mouth became more passionate, more demanding.

To Gina it was as if the heavens opened and he carried her into the sky.

She had never imagined, never dreamt for one instant that, while she loved him, he would love her.

Now she felt her love moving within her like a flood tide.

She surrendered herself completely to the ecstasy of it.

"I love . . . you! I love . . . you!"

She was not certain whether she said the words aloud or only in her heart.

Then she heard the Marquis respond:

"And I love you, my darling, my precious, as I have never loved anyone before."

He kissed her fiercely as if he would make her aware of it.

Then, when they were both breathless, he said:

"How soon will you marry me? I know now that I cannot live without you, and that is something, my precious one, I have never said to a woman before."

"H-how . . . can you love me," Gina asked, "when there are so . . . many attractive . . . beautiful women who are . . . much cleverer than . . . I am?"

"I cannot think of one who is cleverer than you," the Marquis answered, "or as beautiful."

He kissed her again. Then he said:

"You have not yet told me, my lovely one, how soon you will marry me."

"Now . . . at once," Gina said, "or to-morrow . . . in case you change your mind!"

The Marquis laughed.

"Only you could give me an answer like that," he said, "but it is the one I want to hear. We will be married and go away on our honeymoon so that we shall not be here to listen to the gossips chattering, as they will undoubtedly do."

The Marquis had no wish to have people commiserating with him over Lady Imogen's death.

Or for them to say that it was too soon after that affair for him to marry Gina.

He had it all planned out in his mind.

He knew that all he wanted was to have Gina to himself.

He wanted to teach her about love, of which he was aware she knew nothing.

"I will get a special Licence," he said aloud, "and perhaps you can make your Mother understand that you have no wish for a large Society Wedding."

"All I . . . want is to be . . . alone with . . . you," Gina whispered.

"And that is what I want," the Marquis said. "I find it remarkable that we should think the same things and, just as you read my thoughts, I can read yours."

"You . . . are so . . . wonderful!"

They were the words he wanted to hear.

They sat in the Drawing-Room talking and planning what they would do.

Every so often they broke off in mid-sentence so that the Marquis could kiss Gina and make sure she was really there.

Only a long time later did she ask:

"There were no . . . difficulties when you reached . . . Milchester Hall in explaining . . . Lady Imogen's death?"

"The Duke was naturally upset," the Marquis replied, "but there was no doubt in anybody's mind that she died of a heart attack. Only you and I will ever know the truth."

"How . . . could a French General . . . do anything so . . . abominable . . . as to try to murder you?" Gina asked.

"We will not talk about it," the Marquis said. "It is over and we have to forget, just as you have to forget, my beautiful one, that I was such a fool as to fall into the clutches of a woman who was despicable enough to sell information to the enemy."

The Marquis spoke bitterly.

Gina knew he was despising himself for being naive enough to be attracted by Lady Imogen.

She did not quite understand what that meant.

Yet she knew it was hurting him and quickly she put her hand over his.

"Just as . . . you want . . . me to forget what . . . happened," she said, "you must . . . forget it . . . too. It is finished . . . it is over and . . . by a miracle . . . you love . . . me. That is . . . all I want to . . . remember."

"It is all I want to think about," the Marquis agreed, "and I did not realise that love could be so overwhelming, so enchanting."

"That is what I feel too," Gina said, "but then . . . I have never been . . . in love . . . before."

"Neither have I," the Marquis declared, "and that is the truth. So we are setting out on a voyage of discovery, my precious, and I know that what

I shall discover about you will delight me from now until eternity."

Gina put her head against his shoulder.

"You say such beautiful things to me," she said. "There is something I want to tell you."

"What is that?"

"I think my Mother is going to marry your Uncle William. Do you mind?"

The Marquis stared at her in surprise.

Then he said:

"I never imagined such a thing happening! But of course it is the perfect solution. I was wondering whether your Mother would be lonely and perhaps we could have her live with us."

"I think my Mother will be very happy with your Uncle," Gina said, "and if I am honest, I want to be . . . alone with . . . you."

"That is what I want," the Marquis said, "and what I intend to have. There will be no more parties until you begin to find me a bore."

"That means we will never entertain a soul," Gina laughed, "until we are too old and decrepit to see them, and your excellent Chef will certainly give notice if he has no one to cook for."

The Marquis laughed too.

One of the things he adored about Gina was that she could make him laugh.

At the same time she aroused in him sensations he never knew he could feel.

He was well aware of her intelligent brain.

He knew in fact she was everything in one small woman that he had ever wanted, but had thought it impossible to find.

He rose to his feet and drew Gina to hers.

"I am going home now," he said, "although I would like to wait and see my Uncle. But may I come back for dinner? Then I will announce to your Mother that we are to be married."

"Wait until I am with you, because I want to see the surprise on her face," Gina said, "and your Uncle will be surprised too."

"If he too is coming to dinner," the Marquis said, "then that will make us a very happy four."

He pulled her into his arms as he spoke and said:

"All I want is to have you alone and that is what I am going to have as quickly as is humanly possible."

He kissed her until she felt as if the whole room was whirling around her.

Then he put her to one side and without looking back hurried away.

When she went to her bedroom, Gina went down on her knees beside the bed.

She said a fervent prayer of gratitude.

She knew she had been protected and watched over.

Otherwise she would never have been able to save the Marquis from dying from the poisonous drug.

If he had died, there might in the future have been other men in her life.

But there would never have been one who was

167

exactly a part of herself so that together they were complete.

"Help me God to do as he . . . wants . . . help me to make . . . him happy," she prayed, "and help me . . . too, to make him even more . . . influential and concerned in the . . . future of this country."

It might mean, she thought, that she would not have him so much to herself.

At the same time, she loved him enough to know that he was a very exceptional person.

He had shone in the war when he won medals for gallantry.

So now he would play his part in ensuring the prosperity and happiness of England in the future.

She wanted her love to be an inspiration that would spur him on to do great things.

She must not hold him back in any way.

That was Love; the real Love, she thought.

The Love she had read about and which had inspired men and women all through the centuries of civilization.

It was possessive, yet unselfish.

It was the Love that was part of the Divine and came from God.

"Give me the love I give him," she prayed. "And thank you . . . thank you . . . thank you."

Then eagerly she got to her feet.

She must start making herself look beautiful because the most wonderful man in the world was coming to dinner.